MW01165463

White, Christian

A NOVEL BY CHRISTOPHER STODDARD

INTRODUCTION BY BRUCE BENDERSON

TRITON
New York City

ACKNOWLEDGEMENTS

Heartfelt thanks to Bruce Benderson—my editor, mentor and friend. This book wouldn't have come this far if it weren't for him. I would also like to thank David Vigliano, who gave me the opportunity to learn from the greatest. Special thanks to Spuyten Duyvil, Jessica Benoit, Richard Welch of East Village Boys, Ari Fraser, Artem Shcherbakov, Chris Trotter, Jeremy Loughnot, Cullen Bax, Ann Espuelas, David Groff and Charles Flowers. All my love to my family: Jenny Piccolello, Michael Bendlak, Louis Piccolello, Teresa Piccolello and Michael Piccolello.

Author photo by Ari Fraser

Library of Congress Cataloging-in-Publication Data

Stoddard, Christopher, 1981-
White, Christian : a novel / by Christopher Stoddard ; introduction by Bruce Benderson.
p. cm.
ISBN 978-0-9828074-1-5
1. Gay men--Fiction. 2. Alienation (Social psychology)--Fiction.
3. New York (N.Y.)--Fiction. 4. Psychological fiction. I. Title.
PS3619.T64W47 2010
813'.6--dc22

2010028977

*This book is for Bobby because
if he were still here, it wouldn't be.*

INTRODUCTION

Fiction is no privileged shore unto which the writer is invited as a respite for contemplation, no haven for making sense of things. If it's worth the trip, it plunges the writer *in media res*, usually without a life preserver, and challenges him to find meaning and closure in the swirling chaos around him, maintaining the thrill of conflict at the same time. The writer, if he wants to create good prose, has to rub his face in the account and take an unhygienic swim in the murky depths of the unconscious. There is, as well, a Catch-22 that characterizes all fiction: if the material is life-shattering enough, personal enough, to warrant the gargantuan efforts to portray it, how can the writer pull himself together enough to do so, without losing touch with the trauma at its crux?

The most astonishing novels are those that portray experiences that are normally too overwhelming to talk about. Hubert Selby, Jr.'s *Requiem for a Dream* comes to mind, as do some successful novels about the horror of war. Injecting humor into the mix may be crucial if the reader is to be given a way to hold on. *White, Christian*, a first novel by Christopher Stoddard, successfully faces such challenges.

Christian White, the fragile but somehow dynamic protagonist of the novel, is about to go under when the story begins. Young, attractive, droll, addicted, frightened, cynical, homosexual, infantile, campy, sexually compulsive, he's a poster boy for a long list of contemporary dysfunctions. He's a survivor of sexual abuse who finds no intimacy in sex, a boy with a creative mind who can't garner the discipline and energy to develop it. Certainly, his lover, a drug dealer, is no key out of the mess he is in. Nor is his roommate, a leftover from the past whom he handles with contempt and is paid back in kind. His shop-lifting, fashion-victim friends are far from charismatic. His witty, sensible sister is someone he can count on, but getting him back on his feet would get her too far in over her head.

Few novels begin with the protagonist having painted himself into such a corner; still less challenge the reader to deal with such a plethora of alienating personality traits and disturbing, humiliating scenes. Yet there is undeniably something "adorable" about Christian, even as his involvement in drugs pulls him downward into a nearly animal, physically degenerative state. How could the story go on from there? For Christian, the challenge is getting out of the current mess into which he has sunk. We expect to be treated to a series of AA meetings and sessions of psychiatric counseling, ending finally with rehabilitation and self-knowledge. But our hero decides that the only way to leave his troubled past behind is to "take a geographical," as they say in the self-help movement: moving from San Francisco to New York to get out of the situation that has led to his addictions and burying the earlier years under the rug.

What happens in New York is, in some ways, even more disturbing. But by this time, we've gained an intimate knowledge of Christian's family and past, chuckled at some of the perversity of his one-night stands, are privy to the bewilderment and loss that haunts him as the result of his brother's death, and so identified with Christian that we have begun to see ourselves in him and put all our hope in him as well.

White, Christian belongs to a very contemporary and mostly unpopulated genre of novels about the current generation, probably our least articulate generation, and certainly our least literary. Raised on television and the Internet where information comes quickly and easily but accumulates with difficulty into knowledge, viewing formal education as a stepping stone to earnings rather than to an intellectual awakening, most members of this age group are impatient for quick fixes and rewards. *White Christian* affords a very visceral view into such a mentality. Perhaps Stoddard has understood that the best way to show it is as gone awry, with its heart, needs and longings finally peeking through the hipster defenses that have been ripped open by bad choices.

What is more, such a radical excavation of this generation's mindset has accomplished the unexpected. It has tied the novel to a tradition. This is not a "gay" novel, but another in a series begun in early twentieth century with the Lost Generation, continued after World War II with the Beat Generation and barely skimmed by the Gen X'ers, which represent the last time it was seen en masse. It is the literary tradition of social alienation, about the lone individual who cannot seem to navigate the repressions, hypocrisies and unthinking cruelties of contemporary culture, the degenerate individual whose degeneration serves surprisingly as a critique of our society.

Somehow, without sacrificing his own acute perceptions, Christopher Stoddard has intimately depicted the whirling frenzy of a soul with little insight into itself, then put that soul through the sharp-bladed blender of calamity, the only road to this particular character's self-knowledge. And he has made it entertaining and relevant to us. But the most amazing thing about this book is the author's ability to sustain his vision. Rather than appearing as the face of a struggling person peeking for a moment over the edge of a whirlpool, to shout a few words of discovery before disappearing through the eye, he has remained afloat with the character and taken him to a point at which he can squarely face his own past.

Bruce Benderson
New York, NY
May 20, 2010

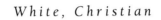

White, Christian

PART ONE

THE SON

ONE

Y ou can feel it when the weekend is over, when the fun stops and you're just acting like a crackhead, at least I can. The majority of the other tenants in the building are hustling to get to work on Monday morning. I can hear the water rushing through the pipes as showers are turned on and off and toilets are flushed. The smell of fresh ground coffee brewing sneaks under the door and tells me that I'm losing it. Apartment doors open and close, people rush down the halls, waves of fatigue and self-awareness flood into me. My "friends" left hours ago. My roommate Philly has gone to work at the French bath and body shop down the street, but not before expressing his disgust, not that he should talk, considering the fact that as a side job he gets fucked for money.

I hear banging on the door. If it's him and he forgot his keys, I'm just going to leave him out there and act like I'm sleeping. I tiptoe toward the door as a second round of knocks sound out like tribal beats, and when I peek through the peephole and discover it's my sister Michelle, when I suddenly remember she's visiting this week and that I forgot to pick her up from Oakland Airport, that's when I realize I'm not just acting like a crackhead. I am a crackhead.

My sister is a unique dichotomy. She's popular, beautiful and as feminine as Alicia Silverstone in *Clueless*. But she also holds on to most of the tomboy attributes she developed in childhood, still skateboarding, snowboarding and playing basketball. The combination of a three-year age difference and the time I've been away have put a space between us that I worry will only grow larger as we get older. Nevertheless I do love her. If anybody were to harm her, I'd kill them, but right now she looks like she's about to kill me.

"Where were you? I was waiting for over three hours." She pushes past me.

"I'm sorry. I forgot you were coming."

She wrinkles her nose in disgust. "It smells weird in here. What have you been doing?"

"I said I was sorry."

She yanks her hair behind her ears the way she always does when she's really pissed off. "You look like shit."

I look down at the dirty carpet like a guilty child. "Thanks a lot, but it's only nine in the morning. I haven't showered yet."

She pulls her cell phone from the back pocket of her jeans. She flips it open and shoves the lit electronic in my face. "It's two-forty-fucking-five in the afternoon, Christian! Where do you get nine in the morning?"

"Yes, it is the morning!" I insist on showing her the clock that I *just* looked at, but the clock has turned on me. The early red-lit digits have mutated into p.m. atrocities. They stand in Michelle's defense, rooting for her and a waning afternoon. I turn as red as the numbers.

"Bu-but it was the morning a second ago."

"More like hours ago."

I plop down on the ground, embarrassed. She sighs deeply then stoops to hug me.

"Just stay away," I say.

My name is Christian White. I'm twenty years old and six feet tall. I have short and choppy dirty-blond hair and dark brown eyes— that's what my mother says, but I think my eyes are black. I have a toned, thin build and am pale white, but my skin doesn't have pink undertones like most Caucasians. There's a faint yellow hue, which most likely stems from me being one-quarter Puerto Rican. I'm also English, Italian and Polish. I'm not anything in particular.

Not that I'm upset about it. Growing up inside the nightmare of living with my mother, one of the few things I looked forward to was her cooking. My mother, Jean White (maiden name Grabowski), made dinner almost every night. In between shifts waiting tables, she'd rush home to cook meals for my brother and me. She made spaghetti with homemade sauce, kielbasa and pierogies, or Spanish rice and beans with chicken. She prepared sausage and peppers, vegetable lasagna and pizza. She fried meat, vegetables and plantains. She baked macaroni and cheese and eggplant parmesan. She experimented with eclectic dishes like hotdog tacos—hotdogs wrapped with American cheese, rolled in Doritos and baked in the oven. When she was running late, my brother and I had a choice of either fish sticks or peanut butter and jelly.

She gave birth to me alone. My father, Andrew Robert White, was annoyed that she went into labor so early in the morning. He sped up to the emergency entrance of St. Vincent's Hospital in Bridgeport, Connecticut, kicked her out of the car and drove off. They divorced when I was seven.

Change is good. It doesn't always feel good at the time. Some people say that it's not the fall that hurts, it's the pavement, but I beg to differ. When you're "falling" from drug abuse, it doesn't feel like falling. I don't even know if it is drug abuse because I don't need crystal, coke, E or weed. I mean, I do them all. As much trouble as I'm having finding a job, I have no trouble finding free drugs.

San Francisco is a Monet painting. Year after year, tourists flock to marvel at its intense landscape of voluptuous hills, trolleys, Fisherman's Wharf and Alcatraz. Alcatraz is a ghost prison on an island close to the bay's shore. Its very existence is a clue to the true face of the city. Even though I live in San Francisco, I never visit the abandoned prison. Tourists come and go. They see gift shops and buy key-chains or magnets for their collections. They take pictures of Coit Tower and peer through binoculars atop Twin Peaks. They walk down my block in the heart of San Francisco and still see the city from a distance.

They miss the fire station on O'Farrell and Polk that's positioned next to Diva, a popular transsexual lounge that's also the hub of gender-bending prostitution. Every night of the week there are firemen on the block, hanging out with the trannies as they fight traffic for a date. The tourists don't see at least one crackhead per block like the residents do. They don't know that one out of every three homeless is suffering from a mental disability. In San Francisco it's easier to get free prescription drugs and a sex change than it is to find a job or shelter.

The police station is located diagonally to the End Up, a landmark night club that's been around since the '70s. It features amazing deep house music and is usually open from Thursday to Monday morning. The club barely closes for four days straight. It's a safe-haven for drug addicts, drug dealers, prostitutes, homosexuals, transsexuals, straights and everyone in between. A person is turned away at the door only if an ID is obviously fake, the drugs aren't hidden well or if he or she can't stand up straight. I've smoked hardcore drugs with off-duty police officers that I met behind its legendary walls.

One Sunday morning back home in Connecticut, while watching TV, I saw a commercial that changed my life. After raging at me for being out until the morning, my mother had retreated to Saint Ambrose Church to confess her sins and pray for my redemption.

I found it impossible to fall asleep despite being awake more than twenty-four hours. My hands were still shaking from the confrontation. I flicked on the television. That's when I saw it: The Academy of Art College in San Francisco. The ad, it said in bold letters on the bottom of the screen, was created by one of its graphic design majors. It boasted an open admissions policy, endless course studies and campus locations scattered throughout San Francisco. I realized what I had to do.

I spent the next two weekends at home. I didn't party or see my friends. I went to work every day on time. Both Fridays I paid my mother the car insurance money I owed her. I helped with the dishes and did the laundry. I went to church three times in fourteen days. The second weekend, I brought up the art college in San Francisco, expressing ample interest in enrolling. I stressed the benefits of the open admissions policy, how someone with my rocky high school record could still be accepted into a good school. I told her how I wanted to become an artist and intended to explore Catholicism while living on the west coast. Impressed, my mother took the bait. She co-signed the school loan, which paid for my first semester and living expenses. I was going to be living in a dorm at twenty feeling like thirty, but I didn't care. The only thing I could think about were the miles between California and my family.

My sister spends her vacation helping me recover from my "weekend warrior" status, escorting me as I walk the streets of Union Square and the Castro, as I apply for job after job at every possible retail and restaurant location.

I lie about my restaurant experience, and I'm finally hired as a food server at Fuzio's Universal Pasta on Castro.

After the interview, I sit with my sister as the sunset sends stripes of light into my living room through the window blinds. Sweat drips from my face and I wipe my forehead.

"Thanks again for all of your help this week, 'Chelle."

She takes a bite of her Fuzio's firecracker pork fusilli pasta. "You're welcome," she replies through a stuffed mouth.

"Last weekend was so fucked up."

She swallows. "Hasn't every weekend been so fucked up for you?"

"No."

But every weekend has been fucked up. I can't remember much of anything that happened before I decided to move to San Francisco, but I can definitely remember what has happened since.

Philly, my best friend from Connecticut, moved to San Francisco to be closer to me, so he says, but I think it was just another thing to do to be more like me. He didn't stop to consider whether or not relocating thousands of miles away from home would be good for him. So mere weeks into his cross-country move, he began to resent me for it. He nitpicked at every little thing I did because he was lonely and missed his family. He instigated arguments when I went out at night without him, insinuating that I was a drug addict and a loser just because I had a social life that involved clubbing, while he sat home watching used Blockbuster DVDs he'd bought and jerking off.

My social life took off one night at a club called Pleasure Dome, where I met a spiky-haired guy around my age named Laurent. The Thursday after that he took me to another club called Faith. He picked me up in a flashy Mercedes, driven by an older patent lawyer named Bailey whom Laurent partied with regularly, and he was also joined by a Filipino drug-dealer named Pineapple. Pineapple was the one who first offered me a bump of crystal. Being a polite Catholic son, I didn't want to be rude. It had been a long time since my weekly weekend cocaine ventures at Gotham in New Haven, Connecticut; my sinuses were tortured by the drug in its shard-like form. I wasn't expecting the pain I felt. I thought I'd feel the same sweet, numbing sensation after inhaling that first rail of coke.

We made a pit stop at Bailey's place before going to Faith. His apartment building was built on a cliff at the top of Twin Peaks. It offered an amazing view of downtown San Francisco. When we arrived, an anorexic-looking woman was making a hasty exit. Bailey introduced her as Mimi, one of his closest friends.

I glanced at myself in the mirrored closet doors that bordered Bailey's bedroom. My eyes were dilated and appeared to be popping out of their sockets. We snorted more drugs, adding coke and ecstasy to the mix.

My heart felt more and more like a dribbling basketball. Scared, I spread myself across Bailey's sofa and took deep breaths.

I pulled the cuffs of my lavender hooded sweatshirt over my hands. My arms were crossed and pressed to my chest, a vain attempt at slowing my racing heart. Without any alternative, Bailey called Cale, his dealer, and explained to him the situation. Since I was on Cale's drugs, he felt responsible for my condition, Bailey explained. Afraid that I'd overdose, he rushed to Bailey's. We were complete strangers, but when he arrived he cared for me like a brother. He sat on the couch close to my head and pulled my upper body onto his lap.

"How long has he been like this?"

"Couple of hours," Bailey said.

Cale, a bleached blond, blue-eyed twenty-something with a decent tan, fished in his pocket for something. Through trembling eyelids, I saw his handful of blue pills. He picked two out of the bunch and asked Bailey for a glass of water. Cale sat me up and handed me the pills. "They're valium. They'll help you sleep."

"Th-thank you," I stuttered. I took the pills and lay back down on his lap. Our eyes met, and, despite my bad high, a warm, fuzzy feeling came over me.

Bailey, Laurent and Pineapple were antsy to leave for the club. I told them I wasn't sure if I was up for it, and Cale asked me to join him while he ran errands around the city. Running errands meant picking up money and dropping off drugs. Despite the risk of being arrested, I accepted his invitation with enthusiasm.

In between stops, he told me how he was from Texas but his parents lived in Tahoe. His father was a retired DEA agent. His mother was a housewife. He had one older brother named Kevin. I told him about my father and my mother—how my mother went crazy after my older brother was killed—inadvertently explaining my cross-country move to San Francisco. I told him about my sister Michelle. He told me about Sean, his queeny, close advisor who worked as his confidante for all his business endeavors and dilemmas. The drug-laced conversations were endless.

I waited in the car when he made his stops. Toward the end of the night, he began closing his eyes for extended periods of time while driving. I had to clap my hands or speak loudly to keep him awake.

Our last stop, as promised by Cale, was in Potrero Hill, which is a San Francisco neighborhood that's isolated by freeways and large industrial tracts. The fog lifts over Potrero Hill before it does in most of the rest of the city, making it a great place for daytime walks. That night, however, the deserted environment seemed to be crawling with dangerous criminals looking for prey.

Cale told me he planned to run inside someone named Nathan's apartment and return in a matter of minutes. I reluctantly agreed to wait in the Jeep. Nathan, another drug dealer and friend of Cale's, preferred he parked around the corner to avoid attention from possible police stakeouts.

The streetlamps automatically shut off. The night sky was turning purple, the first hints of daybreak. I waited. Fifteen minutes turned into fifty. I was beginning to worry about him. What if the deal went bad? What if he was arrested? And why did I care? And that's when I realized I was interested in this guy. He'd left me his cell phone because I didn't have my own. I fondled it, contemplating whom to call or whether I should call anyone at all.

I pressed my forehead against the cold passenger-side window as I stared up the hill at the white duplex that Cale had gone into. My concentration on the house was interrupted by movement I saw in the mirror on the passenger side. There was a man creeping alongside the car. I shifted my eyes to the driver's side mirror and saw another man crouched by the other side. He was sticking a wire hanger in between the door and the window of the car behind Cale's Jeep. I hadn't been spotted yet. Sliding farther down into the car seat, I slowly began making my way over to the driver's side while I thanked a god I didn't believe in that Cale had left the keys in the ignition.

The muffled whispers of the carjackers suggested that they were having a hard time. "Jeep" was among the few words I was able to make out. It was the only one I needed to hear. The engine roared alive. The doors locked automatically. I sped out of the space, paying no mind to the tire that scraped against the side of the curb as I pulled away. I looked into the rearview mirror as I gained distance and saw the two men as a pair of blurry shadows.

I made a right on Carolina Street and then another on 23rd. Once around the block, I spotted Cale coming out of the white house, wandering in the direction of the old parking space. I sped toward him.

"Cale! Cale!"

Giving me a bewildered look, he got into the passenger seat. "Sorry, buddy, fell asleep inside," he confessed, a look of lethargy on his face.

"Did you see them?"

"Who?"

"The carjackers!" I exclaimed, my eyes wide with terror, or perhaps just dilated from the drugs.

After filling Cale in on the details, he had me pull over so we could switch seats. We drove back to the scene of the attempted crime. There were no men. There was no red car. Suspicious of the validity of my story, he changed the subject. I was slightly perturbed by his slumber and insinuation of my hallucinating but was relieved that he was safe and that I didn't get hurt.

Finished with business, he wanted to stop by the San Jose courthouse to pay off a pile of parking tickets he'd accumulated. It was well past sunrise and the courthouse would be open soon. If he didn't pay them by the end of the day, he said, his license would be suspended. He promised that after this quick trip we'd go back to Bailey's and relax. We cruised down the freeway.

I fought to keep him awake while he drove. It became more and more difficult because I was beginning to doze off as well. I watched the cars on either side of us and inspected the expressions on the drivers' faces. One was Bill Clinton. Another was my brother. We passed Mickey Mouse driving. And Cinderella. And Madonna. And Michael Jackson. And Scott Baio from that cheesy '80s sitcom, *Charles in Charge*...

The fluorescent light hurt my eyes as I struggled to open them. I felt woozy and heavy. I lowered my eyes from the ceiling to my body, which was covered in a white sheet up to my neck. A plastic tube was attached to a vein in my arm. Cale's hand was holding mine. He squeezed it. Stitches kept a cut in his left eyebrow closed. He had a large welt on his forehead.

"Hey," he greeted me with hopefulness.

"Hey, where am I?"

"San Francisco General Hospital. I passed out right when we got on the highway. The car completely flipped over, but luckily we're okay. The doctors said I got a concussion. And they say you'll be fine except for a few cuts and bruises. You were very dehydrated, so they gave you an IV. You just need to rest…Christian, I am so sorry about this."

I returned the hand squeeze. "It's okay…Did they find anything in the car?"

"No, luckily I'd gotten rid of the rest of it at Nathan's. I told the police and doctors that I was up late working and fell asleep at the wheel."

"Well, that's technically a version of the truth."

We shared a mild giggle. A moment of silence filled with his regret passed over us. He looked down at the floor. I tugged on his hand. He looked up at me, sad as a puppy that'd peed in the house. I stared into his perfect blue eyes and ran a finger through his glowing blond hair. He kissed me.

"Wait, so you're dating a drug dealer? Are you fucking retarded?"

"It's not like that, Michelle." I glance down at my half-eaten Caesar salad, and one bitten leaf of lettuce looks like it's making out with another leaf, except the other is decorated with shards of parmesan cheese.

She puts her face in her hands. "Do you want to ruin the rest of my life?"

"I know what I'm doing."

"Are you sure? Are you sure you're really going to clean up your act with a boyfriend shoving drugs in your face?"

"Cale doesn't shove anything in my face. He prefers I don't even do drugs, actually, because he doesn't like the way I react to them."

"Where has he been this week?"

"Mexico."

She sits down next to me.

"He's all I have here. You can't trust anyone in this town, not even your best friend. Everyone's a fucking crackhead, I swear to you. Just the other day, I saw some guy who looked like Grandpa in the smoke shop buying a crack pipe."

"Which brings me to my point, Christian, what the hell are you still doing here?!"

"I'm not going back home and dealing with *her* if that's what you're suggesting. I'll take the lesser of two evils." I stand up with my uneaten portion of food in my hand and walk into the kitchen.

"That is not fair. She's not well. It's not the same thing."

"I'm still not going back. I'm sorry you have to be there alone, you know, but hey, you're going to be out of there in less than a year. With your grades, you're going to get full scholarships to plenty of Ivy League schools just like you've dreamt."

Michelle sighs. "Christian…this guy is not good for you."

"He reminds me of my father."

"You barely knew your father."

"Yeah, but from what I've been told and remember, Cale reminds me a lot of him, like a young him."

She gives me a motherly hug. I feel her lean and muscular little arms clenching my sides like a 250-pound wrestler. I close my eyes and want her to hold on a bit longer, but I say nothing as she pulls away, spits her gum in the garbage, walks into the bathroom and begins brushing her teeth. My watery eyes cloud my vision but not my feelings.

"Thanks again for everything, 'Chelle," I yell into the bathroom over the rushing sound of the faucet. She doesn't respond.

"I love you, Michelle."

A sense of dismay passes through the room before she mushily mumbles something.

"What?"

I hear her spit out the minty remnants of her toothpaste. "I said don't fuck up again."

"I won't," I lie and smile.

TWO

You probably didn't know that in addition to being an artist, I'm a poet. Not that it matters because I even forgot I was ever since I moved to San Francisco. Before that though, I'd been writing poetry ever since I ran away at sixteen. I have dozens of notebooks, every page filled. I've never read my work publicly. I think about it sometimes, but Anne Sexton is my favorite poet so I doubt anyone will take me seriously until I kill myself.

I don't want to kill myself, not lately. Since Michelle's visit, and since beginning my new job as a food server, I've felt like new. I can't stop thinking and writing and thinking. I scribble creative phrases on my notepad while I take orders from customers. I write pretty prose next to chicken sausage penne.

My friendship with my roommate Philly is almost back to normal. The week Michelle was here, he slept at his latest trick's apartment. Michelle arranged for the three of us to have dinner before she left, and it went really well. Now that Philly's back, I read my poems to him at night when I come home from work. We pretend he's eating light and healthy with the food I bring him. Usually he asks for the Caesar salad with extra croutons and three servings of creamy dressing, not to mention the bread and butter.

He lies on his stomach in the living room with his bent legs hovering over him. I lie on my back in front of him with my head propped up by a Sponge Bob pillow. My knees are pulled up, and the latest chapter of my life is leaning against my thighs. I leaf through the notebook to find a good one.

He munches on a gooey leaf. "C'mon, just read me one."

"Alright, but you can't laugh at me, okay, because these are all works in progress."

"Duly noted, Mr. Lorca."

I laugh and smack his stubbly arm, with the back of my hand. "Shut up!"

He laughs, too. We're like kids having a sleepover. My tone quickly changes as I try to concentrate on my writing. "The title is 'Perfect Stranger.'" I read it aloud, my voice low and serious.

"That's fierce!" Philly says when I finish.

"Why can't you ever say anything other than 'fierce'?"

"Oh, c'mon, I liked it. You should read your stuff at some coffee houses or something."

"I don't even know if you can call it poetry."

"That's what's cool about it," he says as he uses his hand to wipe the dressing at the corner of his mouth.

"Do you want a napkin?"

"No."

The phone rings. We race to the kitchen but he beats me to it. "Hello?"

His out-of-breath jolliness morphs into a cold stare. "Hi, Cale. Yes, he's here. Sure. Come on up." He presses nine to let Cale in.

"Cale's on his way up," Philly says. He walks through the living room like a zombie, finally ducking behind the bamboo screen that defines his makeshift bedroom.

"What's the matter with you?" I say, standing at the edge of the screen.

"Nothing, I'm just tired is all." He flicks on his television set and pops in a DVD.

"Are you mad that he's here?" I ask as I pick up his half-eaten salad and try to get up the dressing that he dripped on the carpet.

"No. What the fuck are you even talking about? Just leave me alone. I'm tired."

"Okay," I murmur, not knowing what else to say. There's a knock at the door and I open it. Cale walks in and immediately hugs and kisses me. Looking over his shoulder I can just make out part of Philly's face through a chink in the bamboo screen. He's watching us.

THREE

I've been putting my art supplies from the Academy to good use. After spending close to a grand on them, and then almost immediately thereafter withdrawing from the school, I find it comforting that I've found a need for the tools.

I drew this woman, or this drag queen, depending how you look at her. She gazes solemnly at me, tired, holding a martini in one hand and a cigarette in the other. Another piece I worked on involves an extra-large pair of lips with mysterious bluish-gray smoke blowing out of them. I'm sure you can use your imagination to figure out what she's been smoking.

I dream of what I could do with this stuff. Picture me with my own exhibition at one of the trendy art galleries in the city, such as the Culture Cache in the Mission or at HANG right here on Sutter. I'd mount my drawings on the walls, and in between the pieces would be blown-up, college-ruled, loose leaf paper with my poems on them, handwritten. There'd be faint background music to set the mood like Portishead or PJ Harvey. It would almost be a religious experience, as I like to think of myself as a parishioner of the arts.

Speaking of religion, my mother became involved in Saint Ambrose Church when she remarried. I was eight. I began attending their elementary school two years later. The church was at the top of a hill on a busy street in Bridgeport, Connecticut, called Boston Avenue; the school was across the street and parallel to it. My older brother Andrew and I became altar boys. My mother and my stepfather, Michael Alto, became parishioners.

I liked Michael. He was a nice enough man and so was his family. I eventually addressed him as "Dad." He and my mother purchased a home in Bridgeport on Louisiana Circle, which was a nice transition from the close quarters of my grandfather's place.

She planned on changing my and Andrew's last name to Alto, but when my father heard about this, he called her from prison and threatened to kill her and my stepfather if she did. We remained White.

FOUR

"Good evening. Welcome to Fuzio's. I'm Christian. I'll be your server." I try to smile as I balance six glasses of water on a tray.

A guest pushes past me from behind, and it causes me to tip forward ever so slightly. I want to reach out and grab the glass before it spills onto one of my customers, but thirty-six hours without sleep have made my reflexes slow and I miss.

"What-the-fuck?" sputters the obviously gay man I've spilled the water on.

I pull a towel from a busboy's back pocket as he passes.

"Fuck! I'm so sorry," I say.

The man huffs and puffs. "I can't believe this! I can not believe this! I am sopping wet!"

I try to absorb as much water as I can from his shirt and the raincoat that hangs on his chair.

"This is an Issey Miyake raincoat," he says. "This cost me five thousand dollars."

"I'm really sorry, but I'm sure once it dries it will be as good as new." Out of the corner of my eye, I see my boss walking toward us.

"What's the problem, Christian?"

"I accidentally spilled water on this gentleman," I respond.

The gaggle of homosexuals whisper about how in shock they are that this travesty occurred.

"You didn't just spill water on me," the man growls. "You soaked my designer coat."

Something makes me snap and before I can stop myself, I say, "It's water. It's a fucking raincoat. That's what it's for, isn't it? And last time I checked, Issey Miyake didn't sell plastic garments for five thousand dollars."

The customer storms out of the restaurant with his friends, appalled at my reply.

Five minutes later, I storm out…fired.

FIVE

To my amazement, Philly's body sales have become more frequent. He changed his hours to part-time at the bath and body store. Not that I'm upset about it. Whenever he turns a trick, he gives me some of the cash or buys me clothes or food. He believes he's generous because he cares, but the truth of the matter is he does it to feel better about himself. Regardless I accept the gifts. For my birthday, which isn't even for another two weeks, he bought me a black hooded sweatshirt from Hugo Boss. These funds came from his latest sexual endeavor involving a well-known African American violinist from a folk-pop band that I'll call the Don Michaels Band.

Philly now receives weekly checks from this guy, and with the money he's purchased an extensive wardrobe from Diesel, including jeans and T-shirts that are one or two sizes too small, and his ill-fitted outfits look like they were taken straight off a store mannequin. I don't tell him the truth about his new look because he appears to be happy.

If I open my eyes then that means I'll be awake. I won't be dreaming anymore. I open my eyes. My brain now tells my body to stretch and yawn, but my body won't respond. I try again—no response. Fear is making the hair on the back of my head stand up. It feels like a spider is sifting through the follicles, brushing away the strands with each lithe, furry leg. Nothing happens, no matter how hard I concentrate on mobility. I'm just lying here with my eyes open. My face is dug halfway into the pillow. My right nostril's passageway is cut off by the sheet suctioned to it. What if my left nostril gets congested? I won't be able to breathe. I'll die.

"Someone help me!" I think I just screamed, but the sound more closely resembles the voice of a deaf quadriplegic. What if I'm stuck like this forever? How will I live? Maybe I'll end up being paralyzed for the rest of my life, getting around in a wheelchair by blowing through a straw. Well, if that's the case, I swear on my dead brother that I'll use that straw to blow my crippled ass down a flight of stair—wait! I just felt something. My foot wiggled. No, it was just my toe, my big toe. It's wriggling! I'm weeping with joy, but my celebration is cut short because I'm getting congested from the crying. No, I'm not going to die, not like this. I begin violently wriggling my big toe. I'm shaking it and shaking it. Now the rest of my toes are moving, now my foot, now my leg, my whole body is convulsing with my determination. Fuck you! I'm not going anywhere, and when I do it's going to be my decision, not yours! Fuck you, fuck you, fuck you!

A wave of reality flushes through me in the span of a nanosecond. I've awakened with complete body functioning. I make that "Oh!" sound of surprise exactly the way Dorothy does when her house lands on the wicked witch in Munchkin Land.

I rise from my slumber, walk into the bathroom and look out the window at this foreign land. It is no Oz, but San Francisco is just as weird and filled with as many freaks; except maybe here, instead of the poppy field of a heroin addict's dreams, there'd be cocoa trees and a Crystal City.

Stepping out of the shower, I see the black, spotty mold on the curtain, the dirty footprint on the linoleum floor, the smeared mirror. I wrap a damp, used towel around my waist and make my way into the rest of the apartment. My feet feel through the carpet, the finger-toes catching crumbs, dust and cigarette ashes. There are faint black smudges on the walls. The kitchen sink is full of dirty dishes and so is the dishwasher. If this was New York City, I'm sure the place would be covered in cockroaches. Thankfully, there's only one cockroach here. It's the one sitting in front of his ancient computer, trying his hardest to pull a trick or a date. Money or a blowjob, he'll be happy either way.

"Are you planning on leaving the apartment today?" I ask, annoyed. Philly's existence, my association with such a lowlife, reminds me that I'm one, too, and right now I hate him for it.

"Don't worry about what I'm doing," he replies, his eyes glued to the computer screen, his fingers slopping down on the keyboard like digits made of nothing but wet fat.

I spot his "sex-sack" on the hot pink couch, which is really just a cheap Eastpak backpack filled with condoms, lube and dildos (some shaped like an actual-size arm and fist).

"Well, I'm about to clean the apartment," I say. "It'd be nice if you could help."

"Don't tell me what to do. I'm sick of you telling me what to do."

"What the fuck are you talking about?"

"This isn't Connecticut, Christian. I'm not walking in your shadow anymore."

"Uh, I'm asking you to help clean part of the mess *you* made, and you classify that as telling you what to do?"

He continues to not look at me. "Shut the fuck up. You're giving me a headache."

"Fine. You don't want to help. I'll clean up for you."

I grab his sex-sack and fling it over the bamboo screen. The toss gets his attention. He slowly stands and turns to me, acting like he's a dangerous predator zeroing in, but to me he's nothing but an ornery, horny, overweight Sasquatch.

"Pick up my bag, and put it back on the couch." He moves closer to me.

Standing sternly in my towel, I say, "No. If you're not going to clean up your mess, then I'll clean it up for you."

He's so close now that our noses are millimeters from each other. He's blocking the exit.

"Move out of my way, Philly."

"Go get the backpack."

"I'm not getting shit. Now get the fuck out of my way. It was disgusting enough touching your STD-sack once."

I attempt to walk around him, but he moves his bumped, stubbly, flabby body over to the left, continuing to block my way.

"Move," I say.

"Get my bag. You don't touch my things." His voice lisps with anger.

"I'll touch whatever I want if it's dirtying up my house."

I walk forward and he pushes me. The shove is strong and I almost fall. I push him back, but since he weighs almost two hundred pounds, my pushing him doesn't move him much. He swings at me. His fist skims across my chest like a pebble bouncing off the surface of a lake. The shock of my longtime friend attacking me physically abates. I take two steps back and charge at him again, this time the push projecting him against the front door. While he regains his balance, dazed from the counterattack, I take the opportunity to make an escape to my room. I only reach the doorway before he grabs me by my waist and chucks me inside, against the bedroom closet. My towel falls off as my body makes contact with the cold, metal folding doors. Before I have a chance to stand up again, he pounces on me like a rabid boar. He wraps his greasy sausage-fingers around my neck and begins choking me.

"I'm done with your rules and your way and your house! I'd have never come to this shithole of a city if it weren't for you! I hate you!"

My bulging eyes scan the room for help as I struggle to breathe. I see a marble ashtray that's filled with cigarette butts on the edge of the bed. My hand reaches for it. I can almost hear the suspenseful, instrumental music that accompanies a climactic scene during an action film. Darkness circles my eyesight like cataracts, but I get a grip on the ashtray at the last second before passing out. I slam it against his fat head. The impact loosens his grip on my neck, and I gasp for air. Before he has a chance to retaliate, I lunge at him. I beat him in the head over and over again with the ashtray. I keep going until blood is running down his forehead from the wide gash I manage to make in it.

The open wound flashes a memory in my mind of the time I had to drive him to and from Bridgeport Hospital in Connecticut. He had contracted anal warts from an unknown carrier. He had an operation in which the warts were lasered off. When I picked him up from the hospital, he was out of it from the medication. He stumbled into my car, and just before he passed out, he said one thing: "They dilated my asshole to the size of an orange!" I always kept an unwanted yet vivid image of Philly's wounded asshole in my mind. Now, as I stare at this bloody opening on his forehead that I've created, I feel moderate satisfaction knowing there will likely be a permanent scar after the wound heals that'll always remind him of the time he tried to fuck with me and failed, just as he can remove his ass warts but will always carry the human papillomavirus.

He thrusts at me with a feeble arm. I let him move me off him. He stumbles toward the door like a late night drunkard, without saying a word. On his way out, he pulls my small television off of its stand. The second he leaves is the second I feel the pain from my knee billowing up to my brain. I look down. A flap of skin is hanging off my leg like a sick patriotic flag celebrating murder. I must have cut myself when he threw me into the closet doors, which now sport a deep and wide dent and have come off the track. Pieces of white paint have been chipped away to reveal metal underneath. I stand, wincing as my leg straightens.

I lock my bedroom door and lie down on the carpeted floor, even welcoming the crumbs, dust and cigarette ashes that grind into my bare back. My neck is tender to the touch, and my eyes are still watering. My hands shake, and I feel the tightening of my palm as Philly's blood hardens.

No tears of sadness fall from my eyes, though. When a friend threatens your physical well-being, he's no longer a friend and I don't cry for my enemies. The move from Connecticut has changed Philly in some way. I don't know who this man is and, after what he just did, I'm not interested in finding out. Hopefully he'll leave so I can clean.

Never in my whole life have I been more interested in cleaning. I'll begin by sweeping the bathroom and kitchenette floors. Then I'll use the Lysol pre-moistened disinfectant wipes on the bathroom sink and kitchen counters. Mr. Clean will mop the floors. I'll use the vacuum that Cale gave me on all the carpeting. Except for this spot. I want to work around this area underneath my naked body. I want to save it for another time. The next time life gets rough, this will remind me of how bad it can get, the leftovers, the dirt, the residue. This is my gift to myself.

Voices interrupt my melancholy meditation. At least two of them are male in addition to Philly's, and one is female. Two deliberate knocks on my bedroom door interrupt my curiosity. I rise from my sanctuary and creep toward it.

"Who is it?"

"Mr. White, this is the San Francisco police. Open up, please."

I slowly turn the doorknob and let them into my room. I'm immediately handcuffed by a tall, thirty-something, blond-haired man wearing a crisp uniform. I look out into the foyer and see Philly with downcast eyes, pressing a bathroom towel against his bludgeoned head.

"Am I under arrest?"

"That's up to your roommate here, if he wants to press charges. He called us to report an assault."

"I do want to press charges! Look at my head," bellyaches Philly.

"What? *He* assaulted *me*," I defend myself.

"That's not the way it appears," says the female cop. The youngest looking of the three, a black cop, strolls through the apartment with a nosy eye.

The blond cop says, "Why don't you take a seat?"

He maneuvers me by my shoulders onto the hot pink couch. Up until this point, I'd forgotten I was naked. The female cop covers me with a towel before I have a chance to ask for one. Never before have I been handcuffed. The metal wristlets are binding, obviously, but I sense something else. Maybe it's the ghosts of previous arrestees, my sensitivity to their pain. The blond cop introduces himself as Officer Collins, the female as Officer Jennings, and the other male is Officer Cook. He asks me to tell them what happened.

As I'm telling the story of how it was actually Philly who initiated the fight, Officer Collins notices my knee injury, along with four parallel scratches on my right arm.

"Mr. Russo, it appears you've assaulted Mr. White as well. Should he choose to press charges, you will also be arrested."

Looking down at a cum stain on the hot pink couch that the Don Michaels Band's violinist paid for, I tell Officer Collins, "No, no. I'm not pressing charges."

Philly also agrees not to press charges, but I know that it's only because he's worried that I will.

Officer Jennings instructs us to apologize to each other for our immature behavior. She actually makes Philly and me shake hands like we're two disobeying children. I adhere to her request, as does Philly, still bleeding from the head like a runny red egg.

The cops suggest he go to the hospital to get stitches. Philly insists on an ambulance because he feels dizzy, he says. It's too difficult for him to walk the whopping two and a half blocks to Saint Rafael's emergency room. I'm not sure if he's aware of how expensive the ambulance bill is going to be, especially because he doesn't have insurance, not to mention the fact that if he asks me for some monetary compensation for his head injury, I'll laugh in his face.

Finally, everyone leaves. I clean my apartment.

SIX

Still in shock from the attempted theft, I begin putting what's left of my dishes into the dishwasher while Cale and Bailey's friend Mimi rearrange what's left of my furniture. When I'm done with this, I'm going to throw away the litter box and the kitten food. I won't need them since after our fight last week Philly stole Sheba, the six-month-old Bengal stray that an acquaintance of mine found in a Tenderloin alleyway and gave to me.

I had taken her to the vet to be spayed a couple of days ago, and when I went to retrieve her this morning, the front desk receptionist informed me that the owner had already picked her up, which is impossible considering that I'm the owner. Cale promises to buy me a new kitten, but I don't want one.

When we'd arrived back here at my apartment, two of Philly's former co-workers from the French bath and body shop were helping themselves to my furniture, at least what was left of it after he'd ransacked the apartment for everything he ever purchased and some things he hadn't. He'd given the keys to these bottom feeders and told them to take whatever they wanted. When I told them to get the fuck out of my place, these two Frenglish-speaking immigrants tried to walk out still carrying the bamboo wall partition while dragging the hot pink couch. I had to threaten to call the police. Cale stood guard next to me in case either of the two rejects tried to hit me while I spewed racial slurs at them.

I found a trunk of Philly's tacky B-designer clothes in the closet. I tossed them out the back window, which is above a murky man-made pond in the building's courtyard, filled with carp and their shit, algae and rotting water plants.

Not that I'm that upset about Philly kidnapping Sheba and moving back to Connecticut. That cat never liked me anyway. But it's the point of him taking my things that really pisses me off. I'd been expecting him to move out. It's just his attempt at making a dramatic exit that gets to me.

As I rinse off one of the three faux-ceramic dishes with the fruit basket print and place it in the dishwasher, I ask myself out loud, "What am I going to do?"

These past couple of months, Cale has been helping me with my half of the rent. My mother cut me off shortly after I became persistent about not being able to find and keep a job.

"I'll help you," he says while cracked-out Mimi gets distracted from rearranging furniture by a pile of old, assorted fashion magazines in the corner of the living room.

"Do you have any scissors?" she asks while she pours herself a teeny line of crystal on top of Kate Moss on the front page of *Vogue*.

"Why?"

"I have a great idea of what you can do with all of this extra wall space."

"What?"

"We'll make a massive collage!" she squeals with delight, as if she just discovered electricity.

Cale pulls out the vacuum, which thankfully Philly didn't steal. One of Cale's few passions in life, I've learned, is vacuuming. He could spend hours sucking up debris. He often requests that I wait for him to come over when I clean so that he can "have the pleasure" of vacuuming my carpets. He doesn't have carpeting at his place. The floors are hardwood and while he does vacuum those, along with a few throw rugs, it's just not as fun for him as wall-to-wall carpeting.

"I don't know, Mimi. I don't think the building management will like it much if we ruin the walls."

I hand her the scissors. Cale stands the vacuum next to the kitchen counter and walks over to me.

"Babe, don't even worry about it. You've been saying you wanna go back to school anyways, right? I'm always busy dealing, and it'd be nice if I knew you were home whenever I had some extra time to spend with you...It's not like you've had any luck finding steady work anyway."

"What are you saying?"

"Let me take care of you. I'll give you money every week and take care of your rent."

"Why, so everyone can think that I really have been using you all along?"

"Who gives a fuck about everybody else?"

"I don't know, Cale."

"You can write and draw. C'mon, it'll be good for you."

"Yeah, but..."

"But nothing. Just say yes, babe."

I let out a deep sigh, which almost makes me faint. Losing so much breath so quickly feels lethal when I've been up for a couple of days. Maybe I should just try it, I think. I mean before San Francisco, I worked pretty much nonstop since thirteen. I lightly kiss him on the lips and say, "Okay." He smiles, hugs me and returns to vacuuming.

Mimi leaps out of her trance. "I've got it!"

"What?" I ask as I return to my dishes.

"There's this humongous painting almost exactly the size of your living room wall that's hanging in the lobby of my apartment building. Let's take Cale's rented SUV over there tonight and steal it! We can Bedazzle it and do collages. It'll be so much fun!"

"That's perfect. Let's do it!"

"Yay!" screeches Mimi.

"Cale, can I borrow the truck tonight?"

I turn to him for a reply, but he doesn't hear me because of the overpowering noise of the heavy-duty vacuum.

"I'll ask him when he's done," I tell her.

"I'll keep making cutouts for the collage." She scampers off, proud of her idea.

I smile and nod at her, completely forgetting about Philly and Sheba, as if neither of them ever existed in the first place.

SEVEN

I am Penelope Cruz on my twenty-first birthday and Cale is Johnny Depp. Except it isn't just *Blow*, it's also crystal, marijuana, ecstasy and GHB stuffed inside a huge, yellow-tissue-paper-feathered, cardboard piñata shaped like a bird. My friends have done my entire apartment in Hawaiian decor. It seems as if I've been waiting to turn twenty-one for an eternity, but now that it's here, I feel numb. I'm snapping shots of my friends and faux-friends taking whacks at the "polly-wants-some-crack" and thinking to myself that life doesn't get any better. This is it. As my guests scramble on the floor for bags and vials that bleed from a gash in the bird's side, I smile to myself because I believe that this is all I've ever wanted: a boyfriend who takes care of me, a room full of friends and a bird stuffed with drugs. Because I know that in two more years the joyride is going to fade. My hairline will recede. Life will come to ruin me. Year after year there will be fewer and fewer parties. My youth and my beauty will diminish, and then I'll be worthless. I don't know how to be old. I don't know how to act without this attractive curve. Jadedness and bitterness will have consumed me. My past weighs down on me like scoliosis, and soon I'll be a hunchback.

When flushing a toilet, it's not uncommon for tissue paper or excrement to cling to the sides of the ceramic bowl, begging in silence for salvation from the dark lead tunnels, from a morbid water ride sliding the waste into the absolute nothingness of the abyss of raw sewage.

Likewise, I have yet to clean my apartment of the mess from my birthday party last Saturday, which lasted well into Monday. Cale has been gone since Sunday night, following a brief argument we had over the specifics of his relationship with Mimi's husband, Raymond. Lately, they've been spending a great deal of time together. Despite Ray's hetero status and football player-disposition, I have sneaking suspicions about his sexual preference.

For one, he's an avid poet, majored in English in college. We've shown each other our poems. His pieces involve distant people with something to hide.

Mimi's visits to my place have become more frequent over the past couple of weeks, her way of alleviating her loneliness while her husband spends hours with my boyfriend. On weekends, when Cale is away on business, Ray will stop by my place with Mimi, get high and then excuse himself to do "research" online back at their place. The other day when I stopped by to visit them, I had the opportunity to use their computer. When I "accidentally" came upon the history of the Internet Explorer browser, I found someone had spent time on gay hookup Web sites such as m4m4now.com and manhunt.net.

Still, whenever I try discussing this with Mimi, she brushes me off as being paranoid, daring to use the "he's a jock" line while so many jock-types are closeted homos. In any case, it's difficult to take myself too seriously when suspecting Cale is cheating on me because I've been terribly wrong in the past.

Ray's distancing himself from Mimi has forced her into the arms of a hideous lesbian named Erica. Erica resembles one of the mountain men from the '70's film, Deliverance. Mimi thinks no one's aware of her horrid affair, but everyone is. She also thinks I don't know that the primary reason for her recurrent visits to my apartment is not to spend time with me but to smoke my boyfriend's drugs, which are potent and plentiful, though I try not to care because I'm lonely and using her for company, which is not unlike my motives for welcoming the many guests that frequent my home on Sutter Street.

We spend hours cutting and pasting magazine cutouts onto the huge painting that we stole from her apartment building. She works on one half of the painting while I work on the other. Her side flourishes with flowers, bright colors and oblivious happiness while mine depicts a darker, sexier side.

After my birthday party, when Cale disappeared, I thought a lot about my father. Last Monday, I found the email address for the public information office at The Osborn Correctional Institution in Somers, Connecticut. It's a maximum security prison. I wrote an email, requesting information on the whereabouts of my father, Andrew White, a Bridgeport native whom I believed to be serving a twenty-five-year prison term.

This Saturday morning, almost a week later, I receive a reply from the warden, Mark Izzy. The letter confirms that my father is an inmate at Osborn. Mr. Izzy has given me the address of the prison and the inmate identification number of my father so I can write to him. He closed with a solemn "good luck."

I haven't spoken to or corresponded with my father since I was seven. I'm staring at the handwritten letter I've written him. I'm proofreading it one last time before sealing it in a stamped envelope and sending it off:

My name is Christian White and you are my father. I am twenty-one. I live in San Francisco, California. I moved here about a year ago. My mother and half-sister live back in Connecticut. I'm writing to you on my own and I want to keep it a secret, especially from my mother. She would object to me doing this, and I think it would only hurt her and stress her out, and she has enough on her plate. You probably don't care, but just so you know, I love my mother more than anyone or anything.

There have been so many dramatic ups and downs in my life that have challenged me to the fullest extent, and made it difficult for me to keep trying another day. Without my older brother, without guidance from the man who should have been my father, and without any stable relationship, I find it harder to be secure, to conquer my high anxiety and sporadic phases of major depression. I have trouble trusting anyone who comes into my life, and I'm always worried the ones I love are going to leave.

I blame you. This letter is to ask you for some explanation as to why you are the man you are. Why did you destroy your life, and why didn't you think of how it would affect me, Andrew and my mother? I will always feel unsettled, insecure and in some ways empty.

I don't hate you. I've already gotten past that. Since you've never done a thing for me since I was born, I'm hoping you can now. All I'm asking is for some closure, maybe an apology.

I'm working on becoming a professional writer. I'm confident that I will be successful. I'm extremely passionate and devoted to poetry, music and art. Within the next few years, you can bet I'll be on television accepting an award. I hope and pray at least, ha.

I used to be scared of you. When I was younger and living at home, I'd have repeated nightmares that you would hurt me, my brother or especially my mother. But I'm not anymore. I wouldn't let you hurt any of us.

Also, from what I understand, when my brother died, you managed to take half the money from his life insurance policy. I hope you realize that when you did that, you were taking money that I was going to use for college. Why'd you do it?

I put a return address on this envelope so you can write back if you want. I hope you have something to say that can take away some of the hurt and confusion that I constantly carry with me, but if all you would say are lies or retaliate against what my mother told me about you, or if you're planning on arguing with what I just said, then don't bother. This is your chance to help me relieve so much of the overwhelming negative energy I seem to permanently possess.

I'm not saying I want you in my life now. I just want to know why you're someone who's not.

Sincerely,
Christian White

EIGHT

I parallel park on Diamond Street off Clipper at around midnight on a Monday. I'm driving a white, four-door, Toyota pickup truck that Cale has rented for the week. He switches out the car he drives as frequently as possible to lessen the chance of being caught dealing by the police. We haven't spoken for almost the entire ride to Topher's house because I don't want to go. Cale had promised that we would have dinner, watch a movie and get some sleep tonight, but he changed plans when a friend of Topher's called last-minute about a large purchase of GHB.

GHB is a clear, odorless liquid that includes initial effects such as euphoria and relaxation. Within fifteen minutes, nausea, dizziness, drowsiness, visual disturbances, respiratory distress, amnesia, seizures and coma are possible. It's difficult to predict a person's reaction to it. I do it on occasion when I experience a bout of anxiety and paranoia due to extended speed use, sleep deprivation and fasting.

I haven't slept more than thirty minutes since Thursday of last week. I haven't eaten. The only food that my stomach can tolerate after four days of starvation is a chicken-with-cheese sandwich. Despite Cale's lack of dependability, the one thing I can count on from him is an early Sunday afternoon ride to Burger King. It now being Monday, I'm ready for a real meal and some relaxation. But he can never stop working. Whenever a crackhead beckons, he goes. I realize his addiction to work—and speed—is what affords me my apartment, clothes and food, but it leaves no time for us to be together.

The parallel parking has turned out to be more like diagonal parking, but at this point I'm so angry with him and his disregard for my feelings that I don't care. I violently thrust on the emergency brake as he argues with me to maneuver the car properly, and I get out and slam the door mid-sentence. My anxiety morphs into an ugly anger as I stumble down the steep incline of Clipper Street. I hear him in the distance, rustling the plastic bags holding the glass bottles of G as he pulls them out from under the car seat.

My nose pointed to the black, starry sky, I turn the old-fashioned bell that's built into Topher's front door. As Cale trails me from behind, Topher climbs the stairs from his basement master bedroom and opens the door. He's wearing an oversized red T-shirt with the Versace insignia centered in black. His blue jeans are slightly baggy. "Hey bitches," he says.

Cale's voice sounds defeated when he says, "Hey."

"Hi." I greet Topher expressionlessly and begin the walk down.

"Ugh, what's wrong with *her*?" he responds irritably.

Cale shrugs and lets out one of his signature giggles as I seethe from downstairs. "I can hear you two talking shit about me."

Annoyed, Topher replies, "No one's talking about you, you crazy bitch."

"Yeah, right," I mouth under my breath as I enter his bedroom and am met by Pineapple. I say hello. He nods as he exhales speed smoke. Topher has numerous bongs filled with crystal in his house because he likes everyone to have his or her own. By now I'm used to the lack of oxygen. There'll be sporadic incidents of opening the back door, which leads into an impressive floral garden, but it's usually closed due to the suspicions of his landlord upstairs.

Windows Media Player blares an endless round of dance music from Topher's high-tech Dell computer. His guests sit on his bed or on one of the two padded chairs he's put out. The most comfortable chair in his room is a complicated, ergonomically designed black Herman Miller that no one is allowed to sit in except him. He uses it as he works at his computer, a mad scientist mixing music, analyzing financial data and experimenting with the World Wide Web. He sits with Cale at the top of the gay drug dealing food chain in San Francisco.

My fatless ass perches on the edge of the bed as I lean back with an exaggerated sigh. Topher snags his enormous daughter (gay slang for a glass bong) as he falls into his throne. After a couple of hits, he passes the bong over to Cale, who's sitting next to me on the mattress. I feel him giving me a furtive glance to check for signs of my disapproval of his continued drug use into the workweek. I abide by a "weekends only" rule for drugs; however, my weekend usually begins on Thursday night and ends sometime on Monday. But I'm done with partying for now and expect Cale to be, too. My brief moments of sobriety during the week find me either angry or depressed, and I often lash out at anyone who crosses me during such time.

I pretend not to notice that Cale has accepted Topher's offer of speed. I concentrate on the visual effects of Window's Media Player moving in synch with the dance track playing from the computer's speakers. Neon-colored piping streams in and out with the bass. Vibrant greens shoot into spurts of striking yellow, and when the music slows, they become a furious red.

"Gurl, you look like shit."

My daze breaks. "What?"

"You okay?" Topher asks with a hint of concern as he looks me up and down.

"Yes, I'm fine. I stayed home all day. What do you mean I look like shit?"

"Did you drive here?"

I give a snotty reply of, "Yes, bitch. I'm fine."

Cale giggles.

"Fuck you, Cale, like you're fine."

His smirk fades. "I never said I was."

Topher stares. "Bitch, look at you getting all upset. I'm just saying. You need your beauty rest. You can sleep upstairs on the big sofa. I can get you some blankets out of the closet."

"I'm not sleeping here, we're leaving soon," I tell him.

"Hmmph. I don't think either of you should be driving right now."

Snidely I say, "I got us here alive, didn't I?"

"Thank God!" he exclaims as he's leading Cale and Pineapple upstairs to orchestrate the GHB sale.

I skim through a Sharper Image catalogue as I sit and stew. First of all, why the fuck is Cale smoking drugs when we were supposed to eat, chill and get some sleep? Second, who the fuck does Topher think he is, telling me I don't look right? That's bullshit. He just wants Cale to stay here. I know they're fucking. I know Cale is cheating on me. They used to mess around. Topher may give me good advice and help me out when I'm feeling sketchy, but I know it's all lies. I know I look good. I know what they're doing. I know it. I know it.

"I know it!" I yell my racing thought out loud, jump off the bed and charge upstairs. "Cale! Cale!"

He comes out of the kitchen and walks over to the top of the stairs in a rush, worried about my frantic call. "What? What is it?"

"I'm ready to leave."

He protests, "I don't think you should drive."

"Fuck you! I drove here fine. You wouldn't be saying anything if someone else hadn't said anything," I say as I glare at Topher who has also appeared at the top of the stairs.

"Gurl, you're not driving. Give me the keys," Topher butts in.

"Fuck you, I'm going home. You can't keep me here."

He steps in closer, his face hardened into a tough-looking expression. "I'll call you a cab, but you're not driving that truck. Give-me-the-keys."

"Cale, will you tell him? Why are you doing this to me?"

"Christian, let's just stay a little while longer."

"But you said we were going to spend some time alone."

"We will."

My eyes tear from frustration and despair. "Fuck you both. I'm leaving." I turn and yank the front door open. The built-in doorbell jangles from the disturbance as I fly up the steps and begin running up the sharp hill of Clipper Street toward the white truck. I hear Cale's feet stomp on the wooden steps as he runs after me.

My fumbling fingers drop the keys as I try to insert them into the car door. He gets closer to me. I feel like I'm in a horror film, frantic about making an escape from a crazed killer. Reinserting the key into the hole, I unlock the door and climb into the driver's seat. Before I lock myself in the truck, he's already gotten into the passenger seat, GHB in tow.

"Christian, get out of the car. Give me the keys."

"I see you didn't forget your precious drugs before trying to supposedly save my life."

He reaches for the keys, but I've already ignited the engine and pulled the car into reverse. I speed out of my bad parking job and run the stop sign on the busy intersection, prompting a deafening car horn blast from a Volkswagen Beetle I've almost crashed into.

"Are you fucking crazy? You're gonna get us both killed!"

I floor the gas pedal and we race up Clipper. "How are you going to let Topher disrespect me like that? I heard you both laughing about me. We were fine before we got here."

"Pull the car over."

"We had plans!" I exclaim.

"I don't give a fuck! You want to drive like a maniac, you're gonna pull the car over and let me out." His cell phone rings just as a driver behind me flashes his beams. He looks down at his caller ID. He picks it up. "Hello."

I hear Topher's raised voice through the phone. "Put that fucking bitch on now!"

He does as ordered. I steer with one hand, ignoring the screaming horns of the cars in the oncoming traffic lane that I keep swerving in and out of.

"Pull over now, bitch. You see that person flashing behind you?" I look in the rearview mirror and realize it's Topher in his blue Jeep Liberty, chasing me. "You are acting so wrong right now, gurl, and someone is going to get hurt or arrested, which I know you don't care about 'cause you think it won't be you!" he screams at me.

"I'm fine I just want to go ho—"

"You are driving with your lights off with drugs in the car. You are not fucking fine!"

Laughing as if I've kept them off on purpose, I casually ask, "Cale, how do I turn these lights on?"

He reaches around to the left side of the steering wheel and turns on the lights. "Let me drive, Christian."

"Why, so we can go back to Topher's?" I ask as Topher continues yelling into the phone.

"You need to mind your fucking business!" I yell back.

He retorts, "When you're operating a vehicle with no sleep, and my friend who has drugs on him is in the passenger seat, then it is my business."

"Oh, so now he's the only one who's your friend," I say, as I chuck the cell phone at Cale. "Tell him to drive away, and I'll pull over."

Cale says something into the phone, then turns to me. "He said no. He doesn't believe you will."

"I promise I'll fucking let you drive if we go home! I'm not going back to Topher's."

Topher agrees with the stipulation that he stays on the phone, parked a couple blocks away while we switch seats. I find a secluded street in Twin Peaks, a short distance away from Bailey's apartment. We switch seats. Immediately after I hand Cale the car keys, his sweet, worried, apologetic voice changes into anger.

"I'm dropping you the fuck off, and then I'm leaving. You need to get some rest. You're acting like a fucking maniac over nothing."

"Oh yeah? You wanna play games with me, Cale? How 'bout some more?"

The truck door is open as he puts the car into drive. He's already ignoring me, consoling Topher, still on the phone, letting him know we're okay. Furious, I look down at the glass bottles of G. There are two of them, each about the size and shape of the old glass milk bottles from the past that used to be delivered door-to-door. I grab both of them and jump from the moving truck.

"Christian, what the fuck are you doing?" He darts out of the car, leaving the cell phone on the seat.

"This is all you care about, isn't it?" I hold the glass bottles over my head.

"Give-me-the-fucking-bottles, Christian."

"I love you, and this is all you care about."

"Give them to me!"

"Are you just gonna drop me off at home and leave me there?"

"Yes, I need some time away. Plus I still have to run those errands."

"Not any more." Defeated and deranged, I wind my right arm in giant circular motions until I have gained great momentum. After a satisfactory speed, I release the bag holding the two glass bottles into the dark night sky.

Time stops. My arm upraised, bottles suspended, my distorted facial expression, Cale's look of bewilderment, anger and sadness. It all freezes. I step away from myself and evaluate the situation. Has it really come to this?

Time starts again. The glass bottles come crashing down to the black pavement, the syrupy G glazing the street.

"What the fuck!" Cale screams as he reaches for the bottles that have already fallen and broken.

I've thrown away over two thousand dollars of my boyfriend's money. A moment of clarity commences. Shame glints in my eyes but dulls quickly. Tears replace it.

"Take me home."

"Get in the fucking car, you stupid bitch. We're done. Do not call me. Do not talk to me. I'll have Sean drop off some weekly money for you, but I've had it." His Texan accent always comes through in his voice when he's angry or upset.

"I'm sorry."

He ignores me. He picks up the phone from the seat as he gets in. Apparently, Topher has been connected still this whole time.

"I gotta go. I'll call you back." He hangs up.

The rest of the drive home is silent except for the sporadic whimpers that escape my wrecked body. Cale drops me off and speeds away without saying goodbye.

NINE

I can't wait any longer for him to call me. I'm going over there. This is the third time I've called his house and a strange male voice has answered the phone to inform me that my boyfriend is out. I'm almost out of money. I'm out of food. I ate the last of my Top Ramen. It's been four days and still no word.

The walk to Cale's home is therapeutic, the cool breeze, the California sun. If it weren't for these mountainous streets that strain my step, it'd be perfect. My cigarette-stricken lungs are no match for San Francisco's hills.

He rents a one-bedroom apartment on the third floor of a small four-story building in Twin Peaks, not far from Bailey's. I see one of his two latest rental cars parked at the curb. I walk to the gated entrance that blocks me from the stairs and repeatedly press the buzzer until a strange male voice, different from the phone call, finally answers the intercom.

"Yeah?"

"Is Cale there?"

"Who's this?"

"This is his boyfriend. Who the fuck is this?"

I hear static on the other end as the stranger's finger releases the intercom button. I buzz harder.

"Look, he's not here. Just go."

"Excuse me? You better open this fucking door before I break it down! This is Cale's apartment, and you have no right to keep me from coming in. If he's not home then I'll just wait till he gets back."

"Sorry, he said we can't let anyone up."

"Open the fucking door!" I scream into the intercom like a rabid dog that talks. A jogger stops mid-run to stare at the spectacle I'm making.

I yell into the intercom for a few more minutes without a response. I'm not going to stand here while some crackhead freak refuses to admit me into my own boyfriend's home.

A white, metal storm drain is stationed alongside the stairwell. The first and second floor staircases are covered with wire mesh, but the third and fourth floor are exposed. I lift myself up three feet off the ground by hanging onto the gate. Then I grab the concrete ledge of the first set of stairs and climb higher with my feet, using the storm drain.

The rest of the climb, although scary, is easy to do. I depend on the storm drain for support with the left side of my body and use the ledges and mesh for the other half. As I near the third floor, I feel the bolts of the drainpipe loosening with an unsettling groan. Working fast, I shoot my entire body against the second floor mesh as the forty-foot drain comes crashing down onto the tarred driveway. I cling to the mesh like a cat on a screen door, as I pray that my weight doesn't fully rip it with me off the side of the complex. I reach one hand then two onto the third floor concrete ledge and dangle off it for a minute, as I round up my adrenaline-fueled energy to pull my weight onto the next floor. Thinking of that crackhead freak who answered the phone, and how I'm going to wring his neck when I see him, is what gives me the strength I need to reach the third floor opening.

I fold over the balcony and slink onto the concrete staircase, panting and drenched in sweat, less than ten feet away from Cale's front door. With a trembling hand, I sweep the dirt off my black T-shirt. I check my hair and, thankfully, it's still styled to my liking despite the sweat pouring from my head.

I lightly tap the door, a smirk on my face.

"Yoohoo!" I turn the knob, but it's locked.

"Shit, how'd he get up here?" a crackhead whispers.

I knock a little louder. "Open the door, freak."

"Go away, Christian."

"I'm going to count to five, and when I'm done, this door better be open or I'll open it for you."

"Oh yeah, and we'll call the police."

"I'm sure Cale would *love* it if you brought the cops to his house."

"Please just go!"

"One-two-three-four-five! Time's up, motherfuckers!"

I slam my 130-pound body against the thick door four times until I force it back. I hear the splintering of the wood as I rip the lock from its socket. Both crackheads are pushing their bodies against the door to keep me from getting in, but my anger and determination enable this last shove to prove successful when both drug addicts trip over each other and fall back onto Cale's dirty carpeting, which is desperately in need of one of his obsessive vacuuming jobs.

The two crackheads turn out to be Pineapple and Cale's friend Dean, who's visiting from Texas. Dean's above-average build and All-American looks give him a Hardy Boy feel. Pineapple looks like a tanned, anorexic shrimp, but if Dean wasn't too pussy to use his own muscles, then he could more than likely kick my ass. Unfortunately for him, his routine vacation binge on crystal has reduced him to cowering on the floor with Pineapple, both of them in fetal positions, waiting like scared little children about to be beaten by their mother.

"Where the fuck is he?"

"We don't know!" they exclaim in unison.

"When's he coming back?"

"We don't know!"

"Is there anything you do know?" I speak to them like they're idiots because they are. I dramatically pat my forehead with my soiled T-shirt.

Dean speaks up. "All he said was that we could chill in his apartment for a week or two while he took some time off. He said not to let anyone in, especially you."

"Was he with anyone?"

"Just Martin," responds Pineapple with a nasal, island-ish accent.

My body cringes. "Who's Martin?"

"We don't know him. We only met him once."

My voice trembles, "Well, wha-what does he look like?"

Neither crackhead speaks for a moment while each tries to envision this Martin-freak whom they only met once. Dean looks up at me from his submissive state and finally answers.

"He looks like you."

TEN

The two boxes of over-the-counter sleeping pills cost $8.86. Yeah, it's a tacky way to kill myself. I could at least use prescription drugs, but without Cale around, finding anything illegal is near impossible. He supplies drugs for the majority of the gay San Francisco community, and if he's cutting me off, then so will the other twenty dealers I know. Usually I'd be treated like the spouse of a gay Godfather, but not anymore.

I pop each individually packaged pill from the two sheets of twenty that come in each box. The eighty caplets are a buttercup yellow, and I hold them in my hand like I would a baby chick. A tall glass of tap water I clasp in the other. I lift the drugs to my mouth as my cell phone starts ringing. I look down at the tiny, illuminated screen of the wireless device to see that it's my mother calling. Turning from the light, I tip the death-wishes onto my tongue, take a gulp of the water and swallow.

There are times in the night when the floor is on the ceiling and I'm hanging on like Spiderman. When I lose my spider-like powers, I slide down the floor, which has then become vertical. My eyes are crossed, and I laugh at myself while I hang onto the bathroom mirror, singing the song "Back and Forth," pretending I'm Aaliyah.

This doesn't feel like dying. This smells like vomit. This hurts my stomach. This spins my brain and confuses my eyes. This has been a waste of time.

Waking up the next morning, I see that in the span of four days since breaking into Cale's, I've received but two phone calls, and they were from my mom and Michelle. I've eaten my last bit of food and spent the rest of my money on the sleeping pills, so starvation might kill me, but I'm too impatient. There's no way I could wait days to die. It has to be immediate. It was supposed to be yesterday. Rummaging through my dirty kitchen, I open drawers and cupboards. I release Baby Cow from his prison in the cabinet under the sink. My newly adopted, six-month-old black and white kitten was a gift from Cale after Sheba's "catnapping." He's been in there for the past several days and I didn't realize it. He didn't even cry once, or maybe I just wasn't listening.

I find a sharp pair of small scissors on a shelf while Baby Cow charges for his food bowl and eats what's left of his moldy Science Diet. Shit-stink wafts up from the cabinet where he was held captive, and it initiates an encore-vomit from last night's botched suicide.

After kneeling over the bathtub, I point the scissors at my wrist. I'm not pulling a "slit my wrists in the bathtub" suicide. I just don't want to stain the carpet. It's like the story I heard about a teenage farmer who cut his arms off in a tractor accident and ran to the bathtub in the house so he wouldn't bleed on his mother's carpet while he waited for an ambulance.

When I was younger I used to make tiny slices on my arm with a razorblade. I never had the courage to cut deep or close enough to a major artery. This time it's different. There's no option for taking my time. Cale has taken away my time, my pride, my dignity, my security. In less than a year he's influenced my work ethic, drug use, and living and food expenses. I completely depend on him. I have to ask him to pay my bills and feed me like I'm a child.

But I'm not a victim. I remind myself that this is entirely my fault as I puncture my skin. I'm planning on pulling the scissors down the inside of my arm to rip a red river along the way, but I procrastinate. I dig deeper into the same cut, twisting the pointy metal to make sure that I really get in there. It's not so much painful as it is uncomfortable and unfamiliar. It feels weird to have a foreign object reach the insides of my body. It reminds me of the first time I got fucked, which also didn't hurt, but those were different circumstances—the guy had a small dick.

The blood is darker than I thought it would be. It drops onto the soap-scummed tub and washes away circular sections of the Dial residue. I close my eyes and allow the remainder of the sleeping pills' hallucinogenic effects to take over.

In my mind, I'm at death's door. I'm knocking to be let in, to leave here. There's nothing left for me. Knock, knock. Knock, knock? That's not coming from death's door. It's my front door.

"Christian?"

"Bitch, open this damn door now!"

I hear the insistent voices of Mimi and Sean, Cale's "advisor." Maybe it's news from Cale! Frantic to hide my suicide attempt, I grab a damp bath towel from the rack and press it against my wrist, slide the shower curtain over the bloody mess in the tub, and pull down the sleeve on my dark blue undershirt to cover my self-inflicted injuries, and race to the door. I open it and greet my guests with a fake smile after taking in an extra large breath of the apartment's stale air.

"What the hell are you doing in here, gurl? We've been banging on your damn door for the past ten minutes." Sean, wearing a skintight T-shirt, painted-on jeans, and with a woman's purse slung over his shoulder, pushes in. Mimi, with her head down, follows his lead.

"Nothing," I finally reply.

"Hi, Christian," says Mimi in a sketchy voice, obviously cracked-out.

Sean takes a deep breath and exhales, "It smells wrong in here!"

He sets down a Pasta Pomodoro to-go bag on the filthy counter. "Cale had me get you the pasta you liked. There's gnocchi and a Caesar."

"You've heard from Cale?"

Mimi picks up the dry sponge, runs it underwater and begins cleaning the kitchen counter without using soap.

Sean continues to talk. "There's also three hundred dollars in the bag. I'll continue to bring you money until you're able to find a job."

"But I want to talk to Cale."

I turn to Mimi for answers, but she hides from my eyes behind her housecleaning.

Sean continues without remorse. "It's over between you two, gurl."

I never meant to cry in front of company but I'm overcome with grief. "What am I gonna do?" I sob. Mimi scurries over and tries to hug me. I pull away.

Sean responds flatly, "I don't know, bitch. It's just a suggestion, but how 'bout you get a job?"

"Oh, it's that simple, huh? Just poof, I get a job, and it's over? I fucking love him!"

"Well, I don't know about all that."

"I need to talk to him, Sean."

He looks at himself with a Chanel compact and places it back in his handbag.

"I'll see what I can do. Mimi, you ready?"

Relieved that this buzz-killing event is over, she nods and hops to the door. "Call us if you need anything, Christian. In the meantime, eat that food."

"Thanks."

Sean walks into the hall, and as the door swings shut, he shouts, "And take a shower. You smell like shit!"

ELEVEN

Cale's foot smashes through the side of the litter box. When he lifts his New Balance sneaker from the pebble and plastic wreckage, it's covered in shit and chunks of coagulated urine. Baby Cow observes our fight from under the hot pink sofa as he has on many occasions over the past few weeks when Cale has decided that he instead of Sean would check on me.

We started shoving at each other after I threatened to go to the police with information about his drug dealing because he told me he was going to leave me with nothing if I continued to fight with him.

"Don't ever touch me again," I say.

He replies snidely with, "That won't be a problem," and walks out.

I crumple onto the floor in tears while Baby Cow rolls around in what's left of his shit box.

It's over.

TWELVE

I moved in with Cale a couple of months ago, after he cut me off financially and the lease on my apartment on Sutter Street expired, when I had to choose between living with him and his new boyfriend, Martin, or moving back to Connecticut and dealing with my mother. While it seems strange Cale would let me move in with him and Martin after our haywire relationship, he always had a problem with letting go of the past. That's part of why I loved him in the first place. I didn't threaten to go to the police again like most of the tweaking twinks in San Francisco thought. I simply called him after not speaking to him for a few weeks. We didn't discuss any of our old drama. He was the one who mentioned his moving into a bigger place with a couple spare bedrooms, and that I should move into one of them.

The huge loft on Tennessee Street is three floors with three bedrooms, two baths, one balcony, marble floors, and is equipped with all new fixtures and appliances, including a Sub-Zero fridge. My room is on the first floor. Cale and Martin sleep upstairs in the master bedroom, which overlooks the living room on the second floor.

My eyes are lodged deep inside my sunken head, cavernous as the wax cells in a bee's honeycomb. I'm looking upside down and out the window at the buildings across the street as I lie on my back on the bed. The roof of the warehouse looks like the ceiling. My armed father and the police officers are defying gravity. Their lasers target this apartment. It won't be long until they raid the loft. The safe filled with drugs and tens of thousands of dollars is in my bedroom closet. I used to tell myself Cale kept it there because I was the only one he trusted, but now I'm beginning to think that it's because I'm the one he doesn't love—if the cops ever raided the apartment, it'd look like I was the dealer. Martin dangles one of his mini-cameras by its wire to spy on me from the balcony above my bedroom window, and this is when I realize I am alone. I've been awake since Thursday morning, and it's now Monday around 6 p.m. I haven't eaten in days, and there are never any groceries in the kitchen. I've been on this bed for an eternity, practically in the same position, with the fruitless hopes that my absence from the rest of the apartment will attract attention. Perhaps someone will bring me food, or perhaps I'll die. It makes no difference at this point.

A breeze lightly sways my midnight-blue Roman shade forward then back. In between takes, I glimpse my father with cops at hand, looking into my bloodshot eyes from a few yards away. We see each other, connect in a sensual way that I don't really understand. I want him to arrest me, feed me, save me. I wish they would hurry up and break in.

It feels like another hour has gone by, but I'll bet it's only been a few minutes. I hear pounding. Is someone coming for me? Using my last pint of energy, I jump for the door and am about to undo the deadbolt (Cale's installed one on every door in the loft) when my hallucinating eyes realize that it's not knocking, but merely the bass from another tired techno track that Martin decided to spin and then poorly mix.

I hear them up there, their cracked-out conversation muffled by the walls. Baby Cow is stretching his paws under my bolted door and scratching the floor. All I want to do at this point is break his fucking legs. He's making the chit-chat upstairs even harder to decipher. Is it about me? Are they wondering where I am? Am I okay? Am I hungry? I've been asking myself these questions over and over for days.

I reach for my bottled water that's been filled and refilled with tap. My only escape these last few days is quick trips to the sink in the bathroom down the hall. I tilt the plastic to my chapped lips, and one last drop slips onto my chewed tongue and trickles down my dried-out throat. Empty. Fucking empty. What the fuck?

"What the fuck!" I scream as my now 115-pound body flies up and onto its feet as if I'm the new gay character in the movie, *Matrix*. I'm standing on my Ikea bed, my toes are clenching the ripe smelling comforter. I'm so fucking angry. Who the fuck does Cale think he is? Doesn't he know who I am? Doesn't he know what I'm capable of? Of how much I can fuck him back? I'm the one with the power. I'm the one with the information. If I wrote to my father in prison and told him what he was doing, does he even realize how fucked he would be?

My thoughts motivate me to race to the bedroom door. Baby Cow darts away as I swing it open, and I'm running barefoot down the hall past the bathroom. I turn left up the stairs and race to the top on three hops. I quickly scan the living room and spot Martin on the second-floor balcony, smoking a cigarette. He sees me out of the corner of his eye as I make another left down another hall, my sweaty feet slapping the marble floor. And I'm up the flight of stairs leading to Cale's bedroom loft. He's lying on his bed, half asleep.

"What's going on?" I hear Martin's shaky voice as I jump on top of Cale.

I'm wearing nothing but a pair of white boxer briefs. I punch while screaming, "Why did you do this to me?!"

In between sobs and swings, I plead. I'm weak and starving. Tears are running down my face, and Martin is running up the stairs, yelling, "Stop it! Stop it!" Cale rises, furious as a vampire disturbed in his coffin, and pushes me off him. I fall back to the top of the staircase. My head knocks against the base of the railing. He picks up the wooden bat he keeps under his bed. He holds it over his head, his blue eyes dilated. He pauses for a moment, listening to me.

I argue my case. "I'm fucking hungry! I've been starving for days, and you leave me down there to die!"

Ignoring me, the wooden stick does a 180-degree spin, brutally grazing the side of my nose. Blood explodes from my face. Cale's bedroom wall becomes an abstract painting of what's left of our relationship. My head turns to the right, following the bat. The tears mix with the blood running down my face. He drops the bat as his eyes well up, and then we're both on the floor balling. He hates to see me cry, and to see blood. I'm not sure which one it is that stops him from hitting me again. My oily and sweaty body, with my ribs feeling like they're protruding, my dry and burning eyes, and thin, matted hair, he hugs me.

I hear Martin near the foot of the bedroom stairs. I know he's disappointed that our fight hasn't escalated. I know he's jealous that instead of handing my head a trip to the emergency room, Cale hands my hand ten bucks and his car keys so I can go to McDonald's.

THIRTEEN

My new alcove studio apartment on Post Street is smaller than my former place on Sutter. I convinced my mother to co-sign another lease for me, promising her that I'd find a job. After my run-in with Cale at the loft, I decided it was time to move out. Cale paid me a lump-sum "alimony payment" of five thousand dollars.

Baby Cow moved with me for the third time. By now he must be used to my nomad ways, but like a child who's taken in and out of different schools, he's resentful, I sense. But he does appreciate the patio, accessible via the back window, where he's been indulging in his first outdoor experiences, which include what sounds like him fucking other cats.

The bathroom is all new, including the glass shower stall. There are hardwood floors throughout and one medium-size walk-in closet. The main benefit is the affordable monthly rent, should I find a job with an even less-than-modest salary.

The problem now is figuring out how I'm going to pay for next month's rent since I've spent all my alimony on a security deposit, food and three fun-filled weekends at the End Up. I've gone on a couple of job interviews. The last one was on Monday for an administrative assistant opening at a workers' compensation insurance company. I went without having slept and tried to cover my pale, sickly face with bronzer, but I was so nervous that sweat was literally dripping from it and leaking the orange makeup onto my clean white shirt. With wishful thinking, I followed up on the interview this morning. The front-desk receptionist laughed into the phone and hung up after I gave her my name.

"But you don't even have a job yet." Michelle sighs deeply into the receiver like a pervert making prank phone calls.

"I will," I promise.

"You said that before. Are you really making an effort this time?"

"How are you?" I hear the girls cheering in the background.

"Don't avoid the subject with your lame formalities."

"Are you at cheerleading?"

"I'm getting off the phone now."

"No, no wait," I stammer.

My mouth opens to say what Michelle wants to hear. Instead I say, "How's practice?"

I can barely hear her fingers fumbling for the End button because of the deafening cheers of her teenage teammates.

FOURTEEN

I have my father's hands. There's no other part of him that I recognize in me. I contacted him in prison two months ago, and he replied with a letter and a photograph of himself. He's balding, which scares the shit out of me, but what I noticed was his hands. They're exactly like mine, mostly masculine but also a bit feminine. And depending on the angle I look at them, they can resemble dwarf hands. If I'm looking at the palm, they look long and thick. I hate my hands.

*Thursday, April 18th, 200_*
Dear Christian,

I don't know where to begin or if I am going to be able to put it all in this one letter. So please bear with me if you will so that somehow I can answer some, and hopefully all, of your letter's requests.

Thank you, Christian, for your letter, and for your honesty and candor in expressing what you feel and think of me. You have every right to speak that way to me and I expect no less from you. Growing up without me in your life is totally my fault and I alone am responsible. The last time I saw you and Andrew was 1988 (Sept.). I took you both for the day. Our last stop was to get sneakers at a kids' shoe store on the corner of Barnum and Broadbridge in Stratford. You both wanted new sneaks, so it was Adidas for Drew and yours were Nike. I took you to your Mom's house and you guys went to play on the front porch while I said hi to your mom as she was feeding your sister Michelle. It was the last time I saw either of you and the last time I hugged and kissed you and Andrew.

It may have been the last time I saw you both but it was not the last time I kept up on you. Over the years, I have always tried to learn all I could about you two. I have newspaper clippings of your honor roll mention from grade school, I have pictures of you singing in St. Ambrose Church, and I knew you were gay a long time ago. I have pictures of you, Andrew, and me together. I have one where I'm holding you in the air to simulate flying an airplane for you, and another photo of us three playing wiffleball.

Part of my reason for being non-communicative with you or Drew at first was that I was, in my own opinion, not worthy. There is no excuse I can offer, no answer I can give to you, Christian, that will take away any of what you have endured. In no way would I ever badmouth your mom. On the contrary, I have only respect, admiration and a deep appreciation for all her efforts and the love she has bestowed upon you and Drew. I basically left her to the task of raising you both; I would never speak negative of her at all.

I took you both to Beardsley Park one day and we saw geese and ducks. We fed them bread and at one point they frightened you and you ran to my arms for safety. I will always remember your face, Christian, seeking me for comfort and for safety. I got down on my knees and knelt in duck mess, Drew laughed so hard over it. I held you both in my arms that day and Promised you that I would never let you down or let you live a life like I did. The darkness was soon to be upon me. If anyone ever asked me to get high or drink, I was always adamantly negative toward them. I never smoked pot, drank or did narcotics. I just didn't see the purpose and even when I started selling cocaine, I was always immune to the lure.

I started doing cocaine in the early '80s. At first, I functioned well at work and home, but eventually it took over and enveloped me in its grip. Down and down I went and life for me was all about the high. I won't go on and on about it but the bottom line is that I was addicted to cocaine and completely altered by its effect and control. You are twenty-one, so I'm sure you understand the seriousness of the power of cocaine and how it can devastate lives. In no way am I offering any excuses for it, there are no such excuses in my book. Little by little, Our lives were taken apart by my addiction.

You, I am sure, know why I am here and there is no need for details. I live with it over and over, day and night, and would give anything to change what I did that day. I accepted a sentence in 1988 on a re-trial for only one reason: I was guilty and ready to accept society's retribution. Up until that point, I used denial and defense tactics to proclaim my innocence. It was also the point that I, right or wrong, decided to let you, Andrew, and your mom live your life as you were, with your stepfather, Michael, and your new sister.

There are two sides to every story, Christian, and I knew that you and Drew would grow up, and either for hate or curiosity want to hear my side. I counted the years by eating and eating, at one point I was 374 pounds, which caused a myocardial infarction in 1990. I spent time in deep thought as to what was left to salvage in my life. I decided then and there to never allow myself to risk the chance that I would live long enough to be able to answer to you and Drew.

The cigarette smoking I had done since fifteen, the food binges and the occasional high instantly ceased. From that moment, I have not smoked or done drugs or abused my health. I lost the weight. Now I'm fit as any twenty-year-old. I don't desire or miss cigarettes, drugs, or any dependency-related curses.

I was at work on a Sunday morning when I was called to the chapel. It is a bad omen amongst us in here to be called to the chapel. It was a long walk, if not in steps, surely in emotions and thoughts.

When I heard it was Drew I just crumbled, Christian. From every fiber of my being and deep in my Heart of Hearts, I am so sorry you lost your brother. I wish I could take his place and put him back in your life but that is not possible. <u>Please accept my apology</u> for not being there for the worst moment in your life.

You said I was a source for fear and nightmares you had as a child. I am sorry and ashamed that I could cause you that type of fear. In all my years of life, I never wanted to have you fear or hurt from me in any way. There was never any reason for it. I have never done or said anything to you, Drew, or your mom that can in any way have given you reason to be afraid. <u>Yes,</u> I was a very different person away from you three, and I can only assume that some of what I used to do to others had found its way to your ears.

We used to be like the Three Musketeers, from breakfast Sunday mornings at McDonald's to the three of us all cuddled up on the brown corduroy couch as we watched Fraggle Rock.

Oh yeah, one of my favorite pastimes is to write. I write long essays and letters daily. I used to submit some of my writings for publication in the Catholic Transcript. My poetry is a little off the norm. I write poems that have meaning only to me. My forte is the letter. I really do enjoy it and find it easy to do.

I've been here thirteen years now. I have not once in all that time ever stopped thinking about you and Drew! I wish you well my son and am always thinking of you as I have since your birth.

Be Safe, Be Well, Be Happy, All My Love,
Dad

He swears he never hurt my mother. He tells me he's sorry for what he did, that he's a different person now. His penmanship is pristine and feminine. He needlessly capitalizes keywords and underlines requests such as "please accept my apology" to emphasize a point I am not interested in. He believes his abandoning us since early childhood was the best thing that he, as our father, could've done for us. I guess he didn't consider straightening himself out, cleaning up, quitting the abuse and the drugs before going to prison. I believe him not existing would have been the best thing he could've done for me and Drew, even if it had cost us our own existence. Then I wouldn't have to spend a lifetime figuring out how to feel normal, or at the very least how to pay this month's rent.

There's a weight pulling on my stomach muscles like a Burger King meal. There's something else he's leaving out. The relationship he details having had with me and Drew when we were children feels inaccurate. There's something he's keeping from me, and I hide it from myself like the food in a fat man's locked refrigerator or a smoker's nicotine gum. It's as if you're almost there. I'm almost there. The crime he's paying for, and the death of my brother, there's something else. I don't remember the last visits before his imprisonment. I don't remember running to him for safety. I remember being afraid of him. I remember my brother hating him. His infamous reputation that circled us growing up isn't what I define my father by; it is my own memory of him, however vague. But like something revealed in a clearing fog, my past is coming back to me.

FIFTEEN

The sun shines through the windows and penetrates my oxygen-deprived skin as I bask in crystal smoke while slouched on an uncomfortable—yet extremely expensive—designer metal chair in the bedroom of Sean's top floor Nob Hill apartment. His roommate, Rob, isn't home. Rob is the somewhat older Latino friend and mentor of Sean. He taught Sean everything he needs to know about scamming and fashion. They recently leased the apartment on Bush (one block from Blockbuster Video) after Rob served a two-year sentence in a San Francisco minimum security prison for drug possession with intent to sell.

Sean and I have been awake and on drugs for who knows how long, and he's dutifully engaged with Adobe Photoshop, putting the finishing touches on a counterfeit personal check he'll use later in the day for shopping at the department stores in Union Square. Neiman Marcus and Nordstrom haven't even opened yet, but he's already planning a heist.

The idea came up last night when I fretted about how I was going to pay my rent since I have no job and no more boyfriend to take care of me. Sean offered his assistance. Sitting here, I feel grateful for his interest in my welfare, but at the same time I'm uneasy about his strategy to assist it. Not because I suddenly have a guilty conscience. I just don't want to get arrested.

Sunday is a busy shopping day in downtown San Fran. The crowds of ignorant tourists and jaded residents do not exclude Sean and me. We're inside the San Francisco Shopping Center, climbing the escalators in our twenty-eight-inch waist, women's Marc Jacob's jeans. My sketchiness prohibits me from removing my Gucci sunglasses despite the fact that we're inside the mall, and I also fail to take them off at the Nordstrom cash register. My head resting on an arm extended across the glass case, I'm peeking at the old legs of our senior sales associate as she verifies Sean's fraudulent check and then bags the Burberry and Celine bags that he picked out, which total more than a grand.

"Thanks, Mama," Sean, with sass and ease, says to the cashier, and departs with a flutter-finger-wave while I follow close behind with a trembling smile. On the elevator down, I watch as he examines the goods.

Fifteen minutes of power walking later, we're back in Sean's apartment, and he's apologizing to his daughter (the glass bong) for being away and making up for it with long deep hits of her potent crystal smoke. Taking no time to rest, he insists that we immediately go back to the store to return the bags for cash.

I reluctantly walk up to a different cashier. Still unable to remove my huge Gucci's, my hand shakes and so does my voice as I request a return. I'm hallucinating. Suddenly, the sales associate is a nun, looking down upon me as I sin in her convent. A few minutes more of jittery daydreams go by, and then there are two large men coming toward me. They inform me that the bags are going to be confiscated, that the authorities are being notified based on suspected check fraud, and that they can see via the security cameras my accomplice waiting downstairs. Next thing I know, I'm running to the elevators. I power walk to the exit of the building where Sean is smoking a cigarette. No one follows me.

"How'd it go?"

I look over my shoulder as I respond to him with, "They're onto us and fully watching right now."

He stomps out the cigarette butt with the tip of his Dior Homme boot. "Split up."

He is soon lost in the crowd, away from me, away from a failed operation. All my fault. I am left to run on my own. No sleep. No rent money. No friend.

It is weeks later and Sean is different. He repeatedly insists that I'm lying, that I simply pocketed the cash from the purse return. He's weird like that. Of course carelessness can be confused with shadiness, and truth with drug-induced paranoia. I've never claimed to be sharp when it came to my scamming skills.

SIXTEEN

Justice League is on Divisadero Street. I've been attending poetry slams there so I can read my writing to the masses. Poetry has become my new escape. It's less trouble than abusing drugs and just as fun. After the failed stealing, I've been trying to ease off partying. Not that I've completely abandoned going out. Only during the second weekend of every month do I stay away from the End Up and my "friends." I'll spend the night before reading to myself in the bathroom mirror, or I'll laugh or cry another poem out of me.

There's a decent crowd lined up outside the club this evening. The patrons of Justice League are a colorful group, including repressed heterosexual Asian males, oppressed African Americans, overweight Caucasians, and me. Sometimes there will be queens reciting, but I spot none tonight. Most of the time, I come by myself, and tonight I do, too. A veil of rain mists my face as I look up at the congested evening sky and then walk into the club.

A large portion of the poets at Justice often *spit* poetry, which pretty much sounds like rap. The lines resemble lyrics, and these pieces of art are the biggest crowd pleasers. I do receive applause for my performances, but they're considerably calmer than those that follow the musical prose. Tonight I'm going to mix things up a bit. I plan on trying some new material.

A Korean guy reads a comical piece to the audience about the burdening stereotype that Asian men have little dicks. A lesbian complains about her lover's infidelity. Then I'm up. I take a deep, three-second breath and exhale for twice as long, my eyes remaining closed the entire time. The old warehouse of Justice League has stadium-style seating made of wood benches. The low stage is in the center of the room, and when I stand on it, I feel like a ringleader at a circus. The microphone smells like the mix of a thousand mouths. I inhale the ripe odor as I open my eyes and try to relax.

I begin with, "Hi. My name is Christian White. This is 'My Matters to Me,'" and then read the poem. My eyes refocus on my surroundings after I've finished. I've been staring at the people the entire time I've been reciting, but I hadn't looked at their faces until now. The audience erupts into applause, and I'm pretty sure it's genuine. I shake hands with a chubby white guy as he takes his place on the stage, and I return to my seat.

SEVENTEEN

*P*anic Room, *Sex and the City: Season Three, Austin Powers: Goldmember,* and *Star Wars: Episode II* are the four lame DVDs Sean has managed to fit into his extra large, black Gucci bag. Since we're in a rush and he still has to pick movies for himself, I don't want to tell him that he put back on the shelves the ones that I really wanted. Regardless, I know I'm going to pull off this scam better than the last one. This past reading I did at Justice League was awesome, and I'm feeling more confident and less paranoid now that I've been sober for almost two weeks.

"Go outside," he instructs as he discretely calls me on the number pad of his cell phone through the fabric of his jeans.

I pick up my loudly ringing cell and answer with a voice audible to all of Blockbuster.

"Melinda? Hey...What? I can't hear you. Let me go outside." I walk out the front door and through the security posts near the exit that would sound an alarm if I were carrying any stolen DVDs. Sean remains inside and continues to "browse."

I wait about five minutes until he gives the signal. The signal is walking to the window and adjusting his hair in the reflection. He moves closer to the store entrance. No security posts have been placed at the entrance door because there's no handle on the inside, so no one can exit that way.

I swing open the entrance door, feigning impatience. "*Jason,* I need the damn car keys. Melinda is bitching for us to get back. Pick something out or let's go."

He pretends to fish for film rentals for ten more seconds before exiting with me through the unsecured entrance. "Fine, bitch, let's go."

We walk at a normal pace across Bush. I look over my shoulder and notice one of the Blockbuster employees trailing us from behind, his long, stringy brown hair fluttering from the fast-paced walk.

"Excuse me. I know what you did. I saw you." He speaks to Sean, less than two feet behind us, as we strut with excessive confidence. We near the corner of Hyde Street while he continues his pursuit.

I repeat Sean's alias. "*Jason*, what time is the party tonight?" I ask and make it blatantly obvious we're ignoring our chaser.

"I don't know, around ten?"

The Blockbuster man stops following when we turn at Hyde.

"That's fine. I'm calling the police. Don't let me catch you in the store again, either!"

Once out of sight of the employee, we run behind a group of hedges in front of a hospital. Sean takes off his Moschino jacket and sticks it into his Gucci purse. He rolls up the sleeves of his black, long-sleeved, fitted Hugo Boss T-shirt.

While changing he says, "Take off your coat and tie it around your waist. Push your hair down." I flatten my elevated do.

After our quick efforts of disguise, he says we should split up.

"Where should I go?"

"Go home," he says without looking at me.

I start to walk in the opposite direction down Hyde but stop. "What about the movies?"

"I'll get them to you tomorrow," he informs as he slings the designer sack back over his shoulder.

"Okay. Bye."

He doesn't say goodbye. He's annoyed with me. He's been lifting DVDs from Blockbuster for months, and the one time they catch him just happens to be the one time he's taken me along.

I go home, left with no choice but to watch an episode of *Dharma & Greg*, the picture all snowy because of the cheap TV antenna I purchased from Radio Shack.

The ring setting and volume of my home phone remind me of a
screeching bitch, a jilted lover yelling at her ex-beau or complaining
to her friend about her period. My eyes are dry from falling asleep in
my contacts again. The lids, stuck to the orbs, struggle to open, and
I resort to the sense of touch to feel for the receiver like a blind man.

"Hello?"

"Christian..."

"Sean?"

"I need to stop by now. Are you going to be home?"

I rub my eyes and focus in on Baby Cow, who's drinking stale
water from his bowl in the kitchen. He notices my attention, and
with a hateful glance laps up one more sip then hops out the window
to pursue dead plants. He and I never get along in the beginning of
the week because we're both irritable while we come down from the
weekend drug binge.

"Bitch, are you listening?"

I re-focus on Sean's voice. "Yes, I'm here, and of course you can
stop by. Is everything okay?"

"I'll tell you when I get there."

"Are you bringing the DVDs?"

He huffs in irritation. "Fuck the DVDs. I'll be there soon."

He slams down the payphone. At least it sounded like a payphone.
Why would he be calling from a payphone what with the dozens of
cell phones and scammed numbers he's accumulated?

There are no accidents. The waver in Sean's voice conveys this
message to me while he repeats what happened to him this morning.

"I was walking up Post toward my apartment after shopping at
Macy's all morning when I noticed three police cars parked in front of
my building with the lights flashing. Then I saw two cops carrying out
Rob in handcuffs. I think we were raided."

He fills the pipe he's pulled from his Prada clutch. "I am freaking
out right now."

Baby Cow has heard the crunch of the crystals in Sean's crack baggie and has come inside to inhale the secondhand smoke that'll be blown out of Sean's lungs.

"What do you think happened?"

He inhales then exhales the drugs; my furry pet inhales.

"How the fuck should I know? All I do know is that one of the cops there was Rob's parole officer, so I'm sure it has something to do with that. It doesn't matter why they're there. The point is they're there. Gurl, my printers and check paper, and Topher's computer with all the wrong files on it, are still there. Plus, there's a pile of stolen mail in the middle of my bedroom floor.

"This is wrooong," he stresses as he takes another deep, long hit. "Will you get this fucking cat away from me before I kill it?"

I move Baby Cow out of the way with my bare foot. He growls like the crack-cat he is. "What are you gonna do?"

"I don't know."

"Are you going to turn yourself in?"

"I don't even know if they're looking for me."

I straighten the Abercrombie boxers I'm wearing that Mimi's husband, Raymond, left at my old apartment months ago in an unfair, unauthorized exchange for an Armani coat, and I try to focus on the present crisis.

"You can stay here for as long as you want."

"Thanks, but I'm on my way to Topher's. I just wanted to let you know what was going on. I'm getting rid of my cells so don't call my numbers, or they may trace it. I'll have a new phone by tomorrow."

"Is there anything I can do?"

"Yes, bitch. Don't tell anyone about this. Topher or I will call you later and fill you in as needed."

He heads for the door. Baby Cow lies in front of it, a feeble effort to stop Sean and the drugs from leaving my apartment.

"I'm sorry about this, Sean."

"Thanks, me too."

He pulls open the front door, pushing a purring Baby Cow inward, the cat's long black and white fur sweeping the dusty hardwood floor.

EIGHTEEN

Topher and I stand motionless like two streetlamps across from Sean's apartment building, our pale faces glowing atop bodies dressed in dark clothing. We count ten windows up to pinpoint Sean's place, the light in his bedroom left on by investigating police. Either Topher or I have stopped to stake out Sean's apartment three or four times a day for the past week. I live just a couple blocks down the hill, so it's a quick hike to spy. When I've been too high, Topher has swung by in his jeep, looking up the side of the building through the car's tinted sunroof.

"Okay, bitch, we're gonna do this quick. In and out."

I nod my head in silence, an appropriate gesture for any inanimate, electronic object.

"Christian, you okay?" He waves his hand in front of my face. "Bitch, do you hear what I'm saying?"

"Yes."

"Stop freaking out, gurl."

"You sure there's no cops around?"

"Yes, but we're drawing attention just standing on the corner. Let's move."

We walk quickly across the street and into the building, trying to look natural.

The elevator seems to take hours to reach the lobby. An old woman with a French poodle exits the car. She doesn't acknowledge us, not that she could, considering the huge and very dark sunglasses she's wearing. My mouth opens to say hello, but before it does Topher yanks me into the elevator. The doors close and he presses the tenth floor button.

"Are you insane? Don't talk to the neighbors. You want people to remember us?"

"No."

"I should not have let your sketchy fucking ass pop that crystal capsule before we did this."

"I'm fine, Topher. I swear."

"Then mellow the fuck out. When we get up there, do not say a single word. Just get the suitcases out of the closet and throw as much shit as you can grab into them. We cannot be more than five minutes. I'm timing it."

"Okay."

We reach the tenth floor. Topher charges through the dim-lit hallway on his tiptoes. I follow with trepidation. I feel like an eye is watching us as we pass each peephole of Sean's neighboring apartments. I can hear the neighbors whispering into their phones to the police, their lips rubbing against the painted wooden doors as they mouth, "They're here."

Topher takes the key from his jeans pocket and unlocks the door, regarding with extreme care the sound of its teeth as they connect with the deadbolt's notches and turn it open. He faces me and places a sturdy pointer finger over his lips to signify, "Keep your fucking mouth shut."

Inside all the room doors are open. The closets have been rummaged through. The dresser drawers are splayed on the floor. The kitchen cabinets are open, plates and dishes on the linoleum, some broken. Ignoring the rest of the apartment, we make our way into Sean's bedroom. Both printers, Topher's Dell computer, and the stolen mail are gone. We take five seconds of our designated five minutes to mourn the loss of the incriminating physical evidence.

Fortunately, the police weren't interested in the couture in Sean's walk-in closet. We find the two extra-large Tumi suitcases and one medium-size Prada duffel in the back where Sean said they'd be.

Without a word, we grab armfuls of designer clothing and stuff them into the containers. I feel guilty for how rough we're being with delicate Jean Paul Gaultier, luxurious Gucci, Prada and Costume National, to name a few. We fill the bags to the brim with suits, shoes, belts, shirts, T-shirts, jeans and more jeans. We pack bags, purses, satchels, clutches, wallets, wristbands, armlets, Christian Dior makeup and more makeup. I find an old *San Francisco Chronicle* under the kitchen sink, and with it I wrap dozens of perfumes, colognes and eau de toilettes. Topher reveals a roll of silver duct tape, which we use to close the overfilled luggage.

We exit the apartment slow as snails, not in an effort to maintain silence, but because each suitcase weighs more than the two of us combined. We drag the luggage into the elevator, which, as luck would have it, has remained stationed on the tenth floor. My heart is pounding from the drugs, the speed of our packing and the adrenaline rushing through my veins for fear of being arrested.

We pant like dogs on the way down to the ground level, infrequent coughs replacing barks. We're greeted by a deserted lobby, which we run through as fast as we can with our heavy designer burdens. We make it to his car, load it up and drive off.

It takes twice as long to get to Topher's apartment as it normally would because he drives in circles and zigzags to be sure no cops are following us. Sean is waiting at the front door as we pull up. He helps us unload his much-needed clothes, makeup and accessories.

NINETEEN

Yesterday, Sean's mother called to ask why two federal agents stopped by her house looking for him. He told her it was all a mix-up and that he planned on straightening it out as soon as possible. Topher immediately called his own lawyer after hearing that the police were looking for Sean. The lawyer made some phone calls and discovered there was a warrant out for Sean in connection with identity theft, mail theft and check fraud.

He also mentioned that Rob, Sean's roommate, was arrested in the beginning of the week when his parole officer visited, unannounced, to do an unscheduled search of the home. They found about eleven grams of crystal in the kitchen, which they pinned on Rob. The illegal stuff was found in Sean's bedroom. On that day he also left home his wallet where he keeps his license and social security card. Had they not been discovered, the police wouldn't have had proof of Sean residing there.

The apartment itself was leased under a fake name. They paid their first month's rent and security deposit with a check supposedly issued from a major Chicago bank with routing numbers beginning with 1234. Sean picked these consecutive digits on a whim when making the check and it paid off, for a limited time.

His fear of going to prison has prompted him to take the fugitive route. He plans on taking a bus to Los Angeles to stay with friends until the whole thing blows over, but the chances of the charges against him just going away are slim to none. Police are hard-up for identify thieves. Stealing mail is a federal offense as well, and the government does not take these crimes lightly, or so says Topher's lawyer.

Topher was next. For the past few weeks, the police have been doing surveillance at the post office in Noe Valley where he rents out a mailbox to pick up online-ordered shipments of concentrated GHB. They followed him back and forth on drug-runs and pickups, until they raided his apartment a few days ago, where they found loads of crystal, ecstasy, weed and barrels of the infamous GHB.

This isn't the first time he's been arrested, but it's the first time he'll most likely face a prison sentence. His lawyers were able to get him off for the past charges because the police weren't able to produce enough substantial evidence that would link him to his crimes. Plus, he was able to pay off his lawyers himself; his parents never knew of the arrest or that their youngest son was a drug dealer. All they knew was that he was a part-time college student and a part-time medical assistant for a general practitioner.

This time the bail was set at thirty thousand dollars. Sean took a late-night bus back to San Francisco last night to fundraise fifteen thousand dollars, which he did in a matter of hours by collecting from every drug dealer and crackhead who owed Topher money. I'd help him out myself, but I haven't even paid my rent for a couple months. I barely have enough money to feed Baby Cow and myself.

I brought the bail money to the bondsman this morning, only to find that new charges had been brought against Topher, including a raised bail, which was when he decided it was time to call his parents in Colorado. They'll put up their house tomorrow as the collateral required for bailing him out. I left the money with Cale for safekeeping. He and I don't speak, but I reluctantly saw him for Topher's sake. He was evicted from the loft and is now living out of hotels with Martin, who has lost twenty pounds and is stricken with crack sores.

I myself am experiencing an affliction from my Western jurisdiction. The hills of this city I once climbed with euphoria, I now climb with fear. Everyone is getting locked up for their indulgences. We've been eating our dessert without dinner, and the public is beginning to take notice.

TWENTY

Laurent and I are crashing his friend's Volkswagen as I see Topher's number flashing on my cell phone like an alert system that goes off too late. The screeching of the metal Bug as it scrapes against a black limousine creates a weird harmony with the cell's ring. As my jaw gyrates left to right like that of a salsa-dancing skeleton, I answer the phone and try to listen to what Topher is saying, but the deafening crunch of the car makes it impossible.

None of this would have happened if Laurent and I hadn't railed the corner of Sixth and Harrison in a vain effort to be cool as we arrived at the End Up. Wearing dark Gucci's, we'd been staring at the sketchy club-goers loitering outside the place in the rainy grayness of the early, early morning; we peeled around the bend instead of concentrating on the limousine we ended up sideswiping as we invited ourselves into its lane.

Laurent runs from the car to "work" the driver of the thankfully passenger-less limo as I ask Topher to repeat himself for the fourth time because I can't stop laughing long enough to hear what he's saying.

"Are you even fucking listening to me?" he huffs.

"Yes…we just got into a car accident," I say through a chuckle.

"Gurl, this is more important."

"What is it?"

"Sean's been arrested."

Time stops that first second when you realize you're not having fun anymore, when you realize you're mortal and that bad shit really does happen to you and people you know. I'd like to compare this moment of *funlessness*, along with Topher's arrest, to my big brother's death, but I can't because I never had fun as a child; the only difference after he died was that my childhood became even less fun. This car crash that I found knee-slapping hilarious mere seconds ago now just seems dangerous and stupid.

"He's been what?"

"You heard me."

This is the time in my regular Sunday morning routine when the high from the drugs I took forty-five minutes ago should peak, but instead I crash and so does my back on the car seat.

"There are no mistakes," I hear myself say in my mind and out loud.

"What'd you say?"

"I said how'd it happen?"

Topher takes a deep breath. I glance over at Laurent who's now playing the damsel in distress-role for the Mexican driver. A small, cracked-out crowd of End Up patrons stand in psychedelic awe around what's left of the Bug. I try to ignore my racing, crystal-laced mind to focus on what Topher is saying.

"Well, you know how his teeth were bothering him?"

"Yeah?"

"He went to a dentist in Beverly Hills who told him he has periodontitis, which is some kind of gum infection. They had to like go in and clean the tooth under his gums and shit."

"It's from smoking crystal, I bet."

"Do you wanna hear this or not?"

"Go on."

"Anyway, they filled a couple of his cavities, too. He was there all day Thursday, and the bill came out to like a thousand dollars. He went to write out one of his checks…"

"Uh huh…"

"…and the receptionist told him they don't take personal checks, so get this, she said it was okay if he left to go home and get his credit card and come right back. Of course he never did."

"Oh, my god."

"The next day he got caught stealing Visine from a Walgreens in West Hollywood. He was all cracked out. And the dentist, who actually lives in West Hollywood and was shopping there, too, spotted Sean and waited till the police arrived to explain how he'd ran out on the dental bill."

"You're fucking kidding me."

"No gurl, I'm not."

"Oh, my god."

"They ran his name. Well, he at first tried to use one of his fake IDs, but that didn't work. He'd been up for days so they broke him easily. He gave his name after they grilled him for a couple of hours. They found out he had a warrant, and that was that."

"So what's he gonna do now?"

"What do you mean, what's he gonna do now? He's been arrested. He called his mother. Now it's in the hands of his lawyers, I guess. But you know his family has coins so they'll work something out."

"Are they posting bail for him?"

"No."

"Why?"

"He stupidly told his mother that if she bailed him out, he'd run. She's not gonna risk losing her house."

"That's true." I take a sigh as my concentration breaks because the limo driver is now shouting at Laurent in Spanish, which is making the gawking crackheads laugh hysterically. Laurent looks to me for help.

"C'mon, Christian, let's go before he calls the cops!"

"What about the car?"

He looks over the silver Volkswagen before dismissing it. "Just leave it. It's not mine anyway."

"Okay." I exit the car and walk through the crowd toward the club while he runs ahead of me. "What about you, Topher?" I say into the phone. "I haven't even spoken to you since…you know. How did your parents react?"

"I'm fine, I guess. I'm just glad to be out of jail. They had me in a single cell the whole time 'cause I'm gay. My parents were cooler than I thought they'd be, though. Anyways, I'm obviously being evicted, so I've just been packing up all my shit 'cause I'm moving back home to Colorado until this all gets settled. I'll just be flying back and forth for court dates."

I stop right before the entrance to the End Up. I see Mimi wave at me as her unkempt, masculine girlfriend lets her out of the car on the corner.

"So that's it? You're just leaving?" I say, trying to keep the whine out of my voice.

A minute of silence passes between our cell phone lines. It suddenly dawns on me that I've never heard Topher cry. One thing I've learned about crystal is that it numbs all emotions. There's nothing, no state of mind. Laurent told me that Topher has been being drug-tested two or three times a week since his arrest, so I know he's sober; the threat and high probability of going to prison for a couple of years must be resonating deeply.

"Are you still there?"

"It's over, gurl."

"Can I come by? Do you want some company?"

"Thanks, but no. I'd rather be alone. I'll call you if I hear anything else."

I walk along the edge of the curb like you would a tightrope, slip, and stumble into the gutter, where sewer smells waft up.

"I'm sorry, Topher."

"Me too," he says and hangs up.

Mimi runs up to me, giddy as a cracked-out schoolgirl can be who was just eaten out by a Paul Bunyan-type lesbian.

"Hey, Christian, I haven't seen you in forever!"

"I saw you like eight hours ago, Mimi."

"Yeah, but that was like last night!" She laughs like a hyena on helium.

Laurent stands in the doorway of the club, chatting with the cashier. "C'mon, Christian, let's go!"

Mimi looks to me, her eyes like those two X's that are sewn onto the face of a rag doll.

"I'm going home."

"But you just got here, silly!" She jabs me with a translucent, bony finger.

"No, I mean I'm going home."

PART TWO
THE HOLY GHOST

ONE

I'm riding the train home to Connecticut for the first time in two years. It's only been a few hours since I landed at JFK Airport in Queens and took a cab to Grand Central. Because I'm seated facing the back, when I look out the window, New York runs away from me. It's the last week of August, and the leaves on the trees are on their final days of green. I feel like I can see each individual plant cell die where the stem attaches to the branch. Summer fades with the sunset on the city, and as the train races into the darkness of Connecticut, my mother calls my cell phone. I tell her I'll be arriving at the Fairfield station in forty-five minutes. The little bit of belongings I own after selling all my furniture and DVDs via Craigslist have been shipped to her house. I spent the money I made from the sales to buy a plane ticket and this train ride. I'll miss my movies, but I'll start a new collection when and if I ever get settled.

The racing houses blur my eyes until they're too heavy to keep open. I've been as weak as an OxyContin addict ever since I stopped using crystal. My body is withdrawing, and it falls asleep like a narcoleptic any chance it can get, right now being one of them.

I wake up just as the train arrives at my stop. I throw my heavy duffel bag posing as a suitcase over my shoulder and walk out of the car. Half asleep, I stumble down the ramp of the station. I see my mother sitting in her silver Toyota Camry as she digs in her purse for matches. She'd probably be able to find them easier if she took off her sunglasses.

My mother is prettier than most forty-two-year-old women. She looks thirty-two, is of average height, with reddish brown hair, and has a slim figure. Her best features are her almond-shaped, espresso eyes and Julia Roberts smile. The platinum chain and cross she's worn since I was fourteen dangles from her neck as she continues her cigarette-ignition crusade. The interior car light glints off the cross, which pierces a sense of dread and despair inside me. I step to the car and catch her off-guard. She looks up from her bag and lets out a tiny yelp, similar to the kind you hear when you step on the paw of a small pet.

"You scared the crap out of me, Christian!" she barks through the open car window.

"I'm sorry."

Her mouth quivers as it forms a smile. I can see that she's trying to look happy at the sight of me, but I'm aware of what I look like, how living in San Fran has made me lose so much weight and the little bit of color I had in my face. She steps out of the car and pauses before giving me a hug, patting my back. After a few seconds of examination, she starts crying.

"What happened to you? What did they do to you?"

"Mom, what are you talking about?"

"You must weigh less than a hundred pounds."

"No, I don't. Don't be ridiculous."

"Christian, you look sick. Have you been eating!" Her question is an accusation.

"Yes, now can we please just get in the car?"

"Fine. I just haven't seen you in over two years. You look different."

"Well, a lot can happen in two years."

"You've got that right."

I walk around to the passenger door and let myself in. She slides back into the driver's seat and lets out a sigh before turning the key in the ignition.

"How was your flight? I made chili. Your favorite when you were little, remember?"

"Yeah, I like chili."

"It's your favorite."

"I don't remember."

"You just need a home-cooked meal is all. You're gonna be fine."

"I already am fine."

"You're gonna be fine." She mutters a few other comments under her breath that I can barely hear because the rear-view mirror image of my father staring at me from the backseat has left me temporarily deaf. His eyes burn.

"Where is it? Where the fuck is it, you disgusting little faggot?!" He bolts forward, wraps his hands around my throat, and begins shaking and squeezing violently. I can't breathe.

"I don't know, Dad, please," I wheeze. "Please! Please!" I let out a pleading scream and leap from the seat. My eyes open. I look to my left, and my sad mother is gently shaking me by the shoulder. The car has come to a stop.

"Wake up, Christian. Wake up."

I push open the car door and vomit on the gravel driveway. She pats me on the back as my stomach heaves out its contents.

"It's okay, Christian. Don't worry. You're home."

After a dinner that I do not eat, I retreat to my childhood bedroom. During the meal, my sister Michelle hadn't said one word to me except hello and goodnight. She spent most of the meal not eating and whispering the lyrics to a new cheer she was learning for tonight's football game at Trumbull High School. Right after, she left early to go skateboarding.

My old bedroom has the same furniture, but my mother has stripped it of its decorations. Just a twin bed and an old desk remain. The eyes I cut out from magazines that covered the walls have been ripped off. I once kept a black sequin jacket I stole from my mother and a rainbow terrycloth dress from the Salvation Army hidden in a lockbox under my bed. When I was a freshman in high school, I dressed in gothic attire, and it wouldn't be unusual to see me festooned with black makeup, fishnet stockings and ratty women's clothing combinations. My mother took my freakish dressing as a visual representation of my hatred for her. Looking back on it, I think she may have been right. My empty stomach tightens, and I brace myself for another attack of nausea, but the feeling subsides. I lie on my bed, close my eyes and empathize with the transparency of ghosts.

I wake from a dreamless sleep to find my mother standing over me. Her clenched-shut eyes are holding back tears, it looks like. As she attempts to muffle her sobbing, she repeatedly whispers the Lord's Prayer. The light at the bedroom entrance that comes from the kitchen silhouettes her body, like a stained-glass church window. As my eyes adjust to the light, I realize that she's holding a bible and a string of garlic over me. I shoot upright.

"Mom, what are you doing?!"

"Sshh, baby it's going to be okay. Just lie down, relax, and let Jesus wash your pain away."

"Get away from me." I swat at her arms.

She closes her eyes and sways, mumbling the prayer over and over.

"I'm fine, Mom. I'm fine. Things got a little rough for a while, but I'm okay. You don't have to do this. I—"

Something I've said snaps her out of her Roman Catholic trance. She cuts me off. Despair flips into rage. "It's not fine! You're not fine, Christian! Christ, you can't weigh more than a hundred pounds! You're strung out on drugs!"

"This is why I haven't been home in two years."

Her body begins to convulse with deep wails. She collapses on the bed and curls into a fetal position, hugging the bible and garlic close to her chest.

"Mom, I'm sorry. I hate it when you get like this. I hate it when I see you cry."

She falls off the bed onto her knees, stands up straight and stares directly into my eyes. Her mouth pulls its trigger and fires: "I hate you! I hate that I had you! You think I wanted a gay drug addict for a son? If I knew what you were going to become, I would've pulled you out and flushed you down the toilet!"

I stop breathing for a moment, long enough for guilt to glaze her pupils. I slowly exhale, and a tear escapes with my breath.

Her tense body recoils into grief. Trembling, she speaks. "Baby, I…"

I can't say anything. I wouldn't know what to say even if I could. She collapses limply onto my bed. Her lips quiver, and tears run down her beautiful face, which reminds me of the bathroom faucet she always leaves faintly running for the family cat, Onyx. A basket holding the clothes I came wearing is sitting by the door, clean and neatly folded, courtesy of my mother. She rises and holds a wobbly stance as I dress and put on my shoes. Tossing my backpack over my bony shoulder, I walk toward her as if I'm about to receive communion. With my right hand I smooth her tears over her face and kiss her lightly on the forehead.

On my way out, I pass my sister walking up the driveway, and we pause for a moment, not saying anything. She doesn't look surprised, and neither do I. The sound of the house door's deadbolt locking breaks the rhythm of the crackle sounds my feet make on the gravel driveway as I walk away from my family.

TWO

"Tickets! Tickets!" I'm jolted awake. Stomach knotting, I try to decide what to do since I haven't purchased a ticket. It's a weekday. Why not risk riding the train for free? I'd thought. I thought I might blend in with the crowd, but now that the conductor is nearing my seat, I realize my scam will fail.

"Tickets! Tickets! Give me your motherfucking tickets!"

Sitting up, I glance back at the conductor. A monotonous job may be frustrating, but he has no right to speak to paying passengers (well, some of us) like that. I rub my blurry, sleep-filled eyes to focus on the man. He raises his conductor's hat and glares at me. It's my father. He walks toward me down the narrow aisle like Jason from *Friday the 13th*. Pointing at me with a hole-puncher used for checking tickets, he seems ready to cut out my heart with slow, dull stabs.

"Where is it, you diseased cocksucker? Where is it? Give it to me! Give it to me!"

"Please...I don't have it...I don't know where it is."

"Give it to me!"

I shut my eyes as he jams the hole-puncher into my shoulder. He jabs harder. Harder. Harder!

"Son, son."

Eyes open.

"Son, ticket please."

A nightmare. I've been awakened into another. "Well, I don't—"

"I'm gonna need to see your ticket, or you'll have to get off at the next stop."

I stammer out a few syllables. Other passengers are now looking at me. "Sir, I'm sorry. It's just that my wallet was stolen back in Connecticut and uh—"

He cuts me off again: "I've heard a million of these stories. You can tell them to the police officer at the next stop. Now if you'll kindly come with me, son."

"I'm not your fucking son!"

"Keep your voice down." His large hand clasps my bicep. "Please come with me now."

"Get your fucking hands off me! I can stand up myself."

When I stand, my sneakers slide on a small puddle of spilled bottled water, and I fall to my right, crashing into the conductor, who leans onto a businessman working on his laptop. Passengers gasp. I pull myself up and then reach for the conductor's arm.

"Don't touch me again!" He brings himself to his feet by holding onto the back of the seat. "You'll be arrested at the next stop for sure. Assaulting a train conductor is a felony, I'll have you know."

"But I didn't. I slipped," I explain unconvincingly.

"Bullshit. I know a push when I feel one." He straightens his shirt.

I take a look at the businessman adjusting his trousers. He appears to be in his late fifties. Wearing a black, pinstriped suit with platinum cufflinks and an orange tie, he has a full head of gray hair and is attractive for an older guy.

"Sir, I am so sorry for this," I stammer. "It was an accident."

"It's okay." He smiles. "I saw you drop the bottled water while you were sleeping. I'm not surprised something like this happened. I apologize. I should have mentioned it as soon as you awoke."

"No! This boy attacked me, and he's coming with me!"

The businessman tilts his head. "Sir, I can assure you that I am to blame for this accident."

"Assaulting an MTA employee is a *federal offense*!" The flustered conductor takes in a deep breath and loudly exhales.

"Perhaps we can all talk about this more privately by the train doors?" says my savior.

I follow them both. They argue quietly over the situation as I stare out the windows. Suddenly I'm exhausted, wiped out. I wonder if I should just throw myself from the train. Before I have a chance to carry out my plan, the smooth businessman begrudgingly takes his wallet from his coat pocket. He hands the conductor a hundred-dollar bill.

"This should cover the kid's ticket and any physical or...emotional damages."

The conductor slips it into his pocket, nods his cap to the businessman and continues down the narrow walk. "Tickets! Tickets!"

The businessman smiles at me again. "Why don't you sit over here and avoid another nasty fall, huh?"

I follow him. He shifts to the window seat and I next to him.

"I'm Patrick Cullen," he says, extending a hand.

"Christian."

"Just Christian?"

"White."

"Hmm. Okay, religion, race...what about age?"

"I'm twenty-two. How old are you?"

"How old do I look?"

"Oh no, I'm not playing that tired game."

He laughs heartily. "I am fifty-seven years old."

"You seem too happy to be fifty-seven."

"That's because I'm rich. So are you off to New York?"

"Yup."

"Visiting? School?"

"What's with all the questions, Mr. Cullen?"

"Oh, come on. Humor me. I literally just gave you a get-out-of-jail-free card. And please, call me Patrick," he chuckles.

His laughing irritates me. "Yes, you helped me. Thank you. But with all due respect, I didn't ask you to help me."

"I know, I know. You hungry? I have a couple of hours before I get to the office."

"If you're so rich, how come you're riding Metro North?"

"To keep myself humble."

"Ha, whatever that means."

"Have breakfast with me."

I take in a deep breath.

Patrick takes me to Balthazar, a trendy French brasserie in SoHo.

"I've never had a twenty-dollar omelet before."

"There's a first time for everything, Christian."

"Yeah."

"Do you live in the city?"

"I do now." My eyes drift over two tables to where Naomi Campbell is sitting at her business breakfast.

"Runaway?"

"I'm twenty-two!" My body tenses.

"I'm just kidding. So where are you staying?"

"Dude, why do you keep interrogating me? You want to know what the fuck I'm doing here? Fine. I just moved back from San Francisco where I was living for the past two years doing drugs. My abusive boyfriend was a drug dealer, and I had to move out of my apartment after I ran out of money and all my friends got arrested. I tried to go home, but my mother is crazy. I have no money. I don't know where I'm staying. Now can I please just eat this overpriced food so I have enough energy to find a fucking cardboard box to sleep in tonight?" My raised voice garners Naomi's bitchy attention for maybe two seconds.

"Okay okay. Here." He hands me a cloth napkin and I wipe my eyes. I guess I'm crying. Looking down at my whole wheat toast, I notice that drops of tears have washed away circular sections of the butter spread.

"What do you want from me, Patrick? I don't even know you. Why are you doing things for me? Do you want to fuck me? I'm not a prostitute."

"No...I don't know."

"Cause if that's what you're looking for, you're wasting your time. I may be a reformed crackhead, but I still have morals." I start giggling, and then I'm laughing hysterically at how ridiculous I sound.

"What's so funny?"

I pull myself together. "Nothing."

"I've been married for almost thirty-five years. You remind me of a guy I knew when I was in my twenties is all. We were close. My family is exceptionally traditional..." His eyes glaze over with memories of a past love. "So, instead I got married to my best friend and we've been together ever since." An uncomfortable silence falls over our table.

I shove as much egg as I can into my mouth and stand up. "I should get going. I have a lot to figure out."

He raises his right hand. "Wait. Take a seat. I can't let you walk out of here with nothing."

"Really, it's fine."

"Just hold on a second." He picks up his cell phone and asks for the Hilton in Midtown.

I stare at Naomi Campbell. Her extensions are long, brown, and shiny. Her smile and body are, too. Then I catch a glimpse of my weathered self in the mirror next to our booth.

Patrick hangs up the phone. "Done."

"What?"

"You have a room for the night waiting for you at the Hilton."

"I can't accept this."

"You can and you will. Besides, I'm just expensing it." He takes out his wallet and counts out a hundred bucks. "This is all the cash I have left."

"But—"

He checks the time on his Cartier watch. "Damn, I'm going to be late. I have a video conference at nine-fifteen." He gazes at me for a moment and then says, "I'd like to take you to dinner tonight."

"Why?"

"Because I like you." He smiles in a boyish way. For a moment I can see the young man he locked away over thirty years ago. "I have no expectations. Just dinner."

Not knowing how to say no, I say okay.

He signs the bill that the waitress has brought over, wipes his mouth and stands up. "I'll see you at the hotel at seven."

He waves his left hand in my direction, showing me the time displayed on his watch. "I have to go."

"Thank you."

"Yes, and thank you for falling on me, Mr. White."

He leaves. I finish eating my twenty-dollar omelet and tear-soaked toast.

THREE

As he's racing half-dressed to the door, I'm running to the shower to wash off his spit and cum, both of which are smeared and splattered on my face and stomach. It's been a long night, much longer than the amount of time it's taken for Patrick to orgasm and then have an attack of homophobic afterthoughts. I hear the door to the hotel room slam shut as I wipe off the middle-aged semen and try to suppress the shame of a sexual experience that disturbingly reminds me of my biological father. Every time I closed my eyes while I was blowing Patrick, a sinister-looking image of my father flashed in my brain. What was that about? Do I want to blow my own father?

I ask myself these questions as I step out of the shower, toweling dry my face and body. Walking back into the sleeping area of the hotel room, I spot the pile of hundreds on top of the nightstand, and I smile, pick up the bills and begin counting.

Conversation during dinner at Nobu had begun boringly enough: "So, what exactly do you do for work?" and "How was your day?" Patrick sat across from me in his buttoned-down shirt with nine-to-five wrinkles, his suit jacket hanging on the back of his chair.

I was uncomfortable when he'd started merging together casual and sexual conversation, but three glasses of white wine later, I became flirty and obliging. He said he only wanted to blow me, he was amazing at it and dying to do it since he hadn't in years, and as a return on investment, he'd give me fifteen hundred dollars to sponsor my New York City move. Giggling, I insisted once more that I wasn't a hooker as he asked the waiter for the check and I put on my coat.

My hotel room door didn't get a chance to fully slam shut before he began mauling me. He bounced between justifications for his gayness such as "I've never done this before, but it feels so good!" or "It's been years since I've kissed a man," or "I can't believe what you're doing to me. I'm helpless!" I didn't mind kissing him. I was buzzed, and he was not a bad-looking guy, just older. What started to turn me off was his moaning in pleasure like a little bitch while he was blowing me and jerking himself off.

After he came all over me he started crying, and when he left I was happy. Sobriety kicked in fast as I realized I had turned my first trick.

FOUR

I'm working as a receptionist at an investment bank. I live in the roach-infested living room of a sixth-floor walk-up, one bedroom apartment that I sublet from a tattered, thirty-something, black lesbian named Angela. She insists everyone call her by her nickname, Gelly, because of her bubbly personality. But I think it's related to her obesity, how her rolls jiggle like jelly. She's supposedly a graduate student at NYU but she never goes to class. She studied abroad for a year in London and now sports a fake English accent, which I not only find ridiculous but also repulsive. Her weight gain stems from her sweet tooth for Budget Gourmet microwave dinners, half-eaten portions of which she leaves strewn about the apartment.

My godmother is a lesbian. But she takes showers. She does her dishes. She doesn't have greasy, wiry hair that she incessantly brushes, leaving greasy hairballs smeared on the walls, the hardwood floors and the kitchen sink. She doesn't fart while gossiping about nasty cunnilingus on the phone as I try to sleep uncomfortably on a smelly old futon less than two feet away.

Gelly created two walls to ensure privacy for me by stapling canvas to the ceiling that hangs down to the floor. A third wall is the side of the building with a small window that overlooks the tar roof of the shorter building adjacent to ours. The fourth wall is a half of one. The upper half opens into her bedroom. It's been covered with a stapled sheet. We can't see each other but we can definitely hear each other.

She informs me that she won't be able to honor the six-month sublet commitment we had originally agreed upon because she's returning to London to resume her role as a Morrissey groupie. She's dropping out of grad school to follow their upcoming tour, bringing along her old lover whose romance she recently rekindled via international long distance phone calls.

I'm barely making my monthly five-hundred-dollar rent, and now I'll be forced to either find something new or move back to San Francisco. I'm working forty-five hours a week at a crummy job, still broke, with little time or motivation left to pursue my dream of becoming a poet.

It's around midnight on a Saturday. I'm walking down Orchard toward my apartment. I've been to a couple different lounges tonight, spending my last twenty bucks on drinks with the hopes of socializing, perhaps meeting someone, anyone whom I could talk to. Buzzed from one too many vodka-tonics, I relive in my mind the series of choices I made that led me to where I am. I think of the better place I could be at twenty-two. Imagine me as a grad student, successfully pursuing a master's in English, paying my tuition by performing at vintage beatnik bars and selling my chalk drawings at fun East Village galleries. I'm envisioning this fantasy when a man approaches me as I stand spacing out on the corner of Orchard and Stanton.

He must be in his late sixties and is wearing an out-of-fashion white suit. At first I think he's a homeless man, but as my eyes adjust to the bright street lamp, I see the gaudy, expensive-looking jewelry on his fingers and the fancy pipe he's smoking.

"Dreary night isn't it? But not as dreary as you look. I'm Juan."

"Christian."

He grows a sly smile and radiates stamina and confidence despite his age. I find it odd that his name is Juan because all the Juans I've ever met are coffee-colored Hispanics. There's no hint of Latin origin in his face.

"Nice to meet you, Christian. So what are you doing out at this hour? Were you with friends?"

"No, I went out for a few drinks alone."

"Alone? How could any one as gorgeous as you be left alone?"

I ignore the compliment. "Well, I just moved here a few months ago. I would've stayed out, been more social, drank some more, but not only am I broke—"

"Broke? Who's broke, you?" He speaks to me as a man would his grandchild or a puppy. Under normal circumstances, I would've quickly departed this strange scene, but my intoxication and feelings of solitude extend my stay.

We spend over fifteen minutes talking on the corner. I keep looking away from him when we speak, so people my age who pass by in groups on their way to or from the hip Lower East Side bars and lounges won't gawk at this odd combination. No one's looking anyway. After a few more minutes of bullshitting with Juan, he finally asks what we're both waiting for.

"I have a business proposition for you, Christian. You say you're in need of money. Well, I'm in need of company."

I hesitate before I answer. "Listen, Juan, I think you have the wrong idea, I'm not a—"

"Of course not," he cuts me off. "I just want to invite you up to my loft for a drink. I'm offering you three hundred dollars as a donation, nothing more."

"I don't know."

He grins. "Just spend some time with me. I expect nothing."

He has to be lying. My heart is pounding from the adrenaline. Taking risks, being in illegal, bizarre situations with weird men always stimulates a body rush in me, just like the drugs used to. It can feel amazing or debilitating. Caught somewhere in the middle, I remember how Sean would describe the natural high he got when he shoplifted thousand-dollar Yves Saint Laurent purses from Neiman Marcus. I've never considered pulling another trick after Patrick, and I'm scared, but the money entices me to go.

Juan lives on the busy corner of Allen and Delancey. Outside the six-story building looks ghetto, dated. The brick is eroding. Two windows are lit, one on the first floor and one on the third floor. The lobby stinks. Broken glass is scattered all over the floor from a busted window fifteen feet up.

"Watch your step around that glass," Juan instructs. "Pretty sure it was a group of these Chinese juveniles I always see around here," he grumbles.

We ride an old, rickety elevator to the top floor. There are two apartment doors on the sixth floor, but Juan walks past both and into an emergency stairwell. We climb one set of stairs to a door that seems to lead to the roof. He unlocks it to expose a beautiful penthouse, which is completely encased in glass. It's like nothing I've ever seen before. The walls are glass. The ceiling is glass. A steel frame supports the glass paneling. It feels like you're outside when you're in. On the left an open door stands center, leading to a roof garden. Juan flicks a switch and a long, thick velvet curtain extends from the corners of the room, encasing the walls of the entire penthouse, preventing any Peeping Toms from invading our privacy.

He collects 1920s and '30s antique furniture, artwork and design. He tells me how most of it came from California where he grew up, how years ago, after his parents passed away, he had all their priceless household belongings shipped east and refurbished. There's a sofa, curved back chair, and a tufted top stool, all covered in gold chenille. A tall iron-framed mirror rests in the corner of the room. The carpet, circa 1930, is a virtual flower garden, he tells me. To the right· is a circular staircase leading to the bedroom that can be seen from the ground floor. The bedroom comes about halfway across the living space, forming a beautiful glass balcony to gaze admiringly at Juan's collected treasures. There's a grandiose bed, truly fit for a palace. Next to it is a round mahogany nightstand, which compliments the bed's wooden accents. I'm in a time warp.

I'm exploring the bedroom of this rooftop palace when I feel one of Juan's dry, wrinkled hands trace my shoulders and then travel down to my waist before he spins me around to face him, a glass of orange juice in his hand.

"You like screwdrivers? I'm all out of tonic."

"I like screwdrivers."

He tickles my firm belly like you would do to a baby's. "I bet you do!"

I spread a wary smile.

"Why don't you take a seat on that big beautiful bed, you beautiful baby boy?"

"Uh...okay."

He sits next to me, pulling me close with a surprisingly strong arm that I then feel gently travel up my neck, which he abruptly clamps on, and pushes my head into his face. As he shoves his stiff tongue down my throat, I try to ignore the taste of his tobacco-flavored saliva. He throws me onto my back, his unexpected vigor making me nervous.

"I thought you just wanted company."

"I do," he replies with a smile as he hovers over me, taking my chin in his left hand. "And you just want my money, don't you?"

"Yeah, but, I'm not a prosti—"

He cuts me off with a hard slap across the face. "You spoiled fucking kids these days! You think you can always get something for nothing! Well, you're not going to get anything if you don't start behaving!"

My body cringes, startled. I hold my assaulted face in my hands. He stands at the end of the bed, staring me down like a disappointed parent.

"Now. To whom were you addressing inappropriately?"

"Huh? I don't know what—"

"Master! Say it, you fucking faggot!"

My eyes brim with tears. "Master?"

"Good boy," he congratulates as he wiggles my kneecap. He then walks over to the nightstand to take a swig of his drink.

I rise to my feet. "I'm sorry. I don't think I'm comfortable with this."

He chucks his drink at the thick glass wall. It shatters. He charges at me with a raging hard-on that's made a tent of his dress pants.

"Don't play games with me. Your time is bought. Now turn the fuck around and take off those trousers!"

He continues to scold me, an erect pointer finger less than a centimeter from my nose. Frightened and confused, I do as he says. Is this role-play or is he serious? He pulls me down onto his lap and begins spanking me.

"Say you're sorry."

"What?"

"Say it!" Before I can follow his order, he pounds his fist into my back so hard I lose my breath for what feels like an eternity.

"Say you're sorry. Say you're very sorry now!"

The adrenaline running through my veins gives me the strength to pull myself off him.

"I'm leaving!"

"The hell you are!"

My stomach in knots, I turn to face him and fight, but all I see is his fist coming at me and then nothing.

FIVE

Lately, I see time as still life. Years pass, I get older, my problems become more dramatic, but they all share distinct similarities and the same unsolved foundations from when I was fourteen years old. I wonder if life was created to amuse someone observing from above, as a joke. Sometimes I feel like each earthbound creature was birth-rited a specific question, such as a permanent, unsolved issue that had to be either answered or not by his or her time of death. Like a fucked up game. Like life is either win or lose before we even know the rules, before we get to know ourselves. I ponder the unanswered, consider the possibilities. If my theory is fact, then is there a second level? If I win life, if I solve my problems and die, I ask, what next? If I lose then what won't be? Am I just a game piece? Are we instruments of some god's entertainment? Such ridiculous ideas, I tell myself right about now, before I begin to realize, before I never meet motivation again, before I begin to lose.

The first thing I remember about San Francisco is that it smells like shit, and not metaphorically. You get sporadic whiffs of it as you walk the city streets. The stench emanates from the sewers as a result of the city's horrible sewage system. One night something exploded in the drain next to Cale's driveway. In the morning there was a whole piece of human feces laid out like a large, dead rat.

This all comes to mind in my dream, as I'm laid out on my right side in front of a gutter on the corner of Mason and Polk. My arm is reaching into it as far as it can go. I'm shirtless and covered in small cuts and bruises. There are no cars or people on the street. There's no one to stop and gawk at the scene I'm making. Overwhelmed with desperation, I keep feeling down into the shithole. I'm crying out of frustration. I scream out to no one.

"Someone help me! I know it's in here somewhere! That's where he left it! Please! Please!" Pulling back to rest for a second, I sit cross-legged and sob in my lap. I hear a voice off in the distance, replying to my plea.

"Here! I'm coming!" A figure of a man, shadowed by the tall street lamps, grows bigger and bigger as it runs up from Market Street. As he nears, I vaguely recognize him only from the photo albums my mother hid under her bed when I was younger. He looks the same age as me, which is impossible since he's twenty years older. He asks, "Did you find it? Did you find it?!"

I'm speechless. Suddenly the lights turn on in the Jack in the Box restaurant in front of me. Cars whiz by, and people walk down the street, staring at the two of us with extreme curiosity.

"Did you find it? Did you fucking find it, you little faggot?!" He grabs me by the throat. "I am going to ask you one more fucking time, and then I'm going to fucking bury you. Did. You. Find. It?" His grip on my neck tightens, and I start to lose consciousness.

Before I faint, I respond carefully, "Did I find what, Dad?"

Gelly's shrill voice with the fake London accent wakes me as she gabs on the phone about The Smiths and cunnilingus. I stare for awhile at the ceiling in the living room I call a bedroom before I push my body up with my hands in an effort to sit. The weight on my ass causes excruciating pain, and I'm forced to lie back down.

What happened? I remember drinking alone, the walk home, and Juan. I remember going to his penthouse where he got rough and I got scared. I remember him hitting me. And then nothing.

Tears bead on my oily face. I mouth, "What happened," and that's when I feel my bottom lip is swollen. I raise my finger to examine it, but it's too tender to touch. I stumble to the bathroom for a more thorough inspection.

I flick on the overhead fluorescent light just in time to see a huge cockroach scurry down the drain of the bathroom sink. I'll kill it if it has the balls to come back. Do cockroaches even have balls? It could also be a female, but how could I tell?

I'm wearing the same clothes I had on last night, a black Rogan T-shirt and jeans. The T-shirt is torn across the chest. The front of my light blue jeans are clean. I turn around to inspect the rear to find a dark red stain growing on the ass. Blood from last night, brown and hardened, has begun to mix with a wet, deep red version that must have started when I walked from the living room to here. Every move I make is a thousand needles poking inside my asshole. A wad of stained cash sticks out of a back pocket.

I rip off my shirt with trembling hands. I shut my eyes before looking at my bare chest. When I open them, I see nothing but a smooth, slim figure. When I turn around, though, I see that bruises and welts litter my back.

I've been avoiding looking at my face. Turning to the mirror, I see a monster growling back at me. My eyes are bloodshot. I have a cut on my right eyebrow that was probably caused by one of the times Juan punched me. The reason I know it was more than once is because I also have a shiner, ugly and purple, under my left eye.

What do I do? Should I go to the hospital and call the police? If I do, what am I going to tell them, a weird guy named Juan in a white suit propositioned me on the street, took me back to his place and raped me after I'd already agreed to be paid for sex? I don't even know if he raped me because, "I can't remember!"

"Christian, what in bloody hell are you doing in there, mate? I'm trying to talk to my bird!"

Through heaves of tears I say to her, "I'm sorry, Gelly. You know me, always talking to myself."

"Can't you talk to yourself quietly?"

Three days later. I told Gelly during grocery shopping last night that my injuries were the result of a mugging. I told the doctor at the walk-in clinic the same story, and he prescribed me antibiotics and painkillers for the injuries to my torso, which I hope also work on the cuts in my asshole. Both the doctor and Gelly bought my story, as did the people at my job when I told them this morning. I'm back at work, hardly working, trying to find a comfortable way to sit without putting pressure where it hurts, browsing the Internet. I go onto the *New York Post* Web site and immediately click on *Page Six*, the gossip column. There's always some version of the truth about celebrities and various high-end humans. After *Page Six*, I turn to Cindy Adams, who always spills the steaming hot tea of gossip and upcoming scandals before the rest of the news world's water is even boiling. If I have time after having my fill of useless information, I debate on whether or not I should read the real news. I skim through the local headlines: *Bloody Bowery, Bronx Triple Horror, Pay For "Mafia" Judge, New Jersey Mom: 2 Kids Brutally Slain, No Leads In Brutal Homicide Of Eccentric Architect, Shark Girl A Big Hit.*

I click on the shark girl story and read about how Bethany Hamilton, the young Hawaiian surfer who lost her limb in a shark attack, threw out the first pitch at Yankee Stadium last night. Then I backtrack to the previous article about the architect murder. Suddenly the salad I ate at lunch turns in my stomach. My heart starts beating faster and I struggle for air. My hands start shaking. My co-worker looks up from her electronic daze to ask me if I'm okay. Sweat instantly beads on my forehead.

"I'm fine."

"You don't look fine."

"Yes, I'm fine." I quickly minimize the screen I'm reading on my computer as if she knew or even cared about my unwelcome discovery. My stomach gurgles and my insides rise. I dart toward the bathroom. "I'll be right back."

I swing open the bathroom door, nearly take out an exiting employee, race to a toilet stall and fall to my knees. Praying to the toilet seat, I give offering after offering of acid-washed, greenish vomit. My sinuses burn as they flood with bile.

About five minutes later I'm blowing the leftovers out of my nose as I quietly weep. I hear a knock on the stall door.

"Yeah?"

A deep voice I don't recognize speaks. "You okay in there, man?"

"Yes. Thank you."

"You sure?"

Exasperated, I repeat myself. "Yes. Thank you."

"Okay."

"Food poisoning...I think it was the chicken I had for lunch."

After I hear the man exit the restroom, I come out of the stall and analyze myself in the large mirror. My eyes are bloodshot and puffy. My tie, now askew, has a small splodge of throw-up near the tip. I turn on the faucet and rinse my face and tie with cold water. I brush my hair back with my hands and adjust my outfit. Taking a deep breath, I leave the bathroom and return to my desk to reread the proof of my ill-fated future:

Juan Carlos, 75, the famous architectural designer, was found by cops at 9:33 a.m., Saturday, lying face down and naked in bed in his inimitable glass penthouse in the Lower East Side of Manhattan, located on the corner of Allen and Delancey. He was discovered by one of his personal assistants, who checked on him after he hadn't shown up at the studio for almost a week. She called police when she noticed an odor that seemed to be coming through the front door.

A spokeswoman for the Medical Examiner's Office said Mr. Carlos was a homicide victim who died from blunt-impact trauma to the chest, neck and ribs, and a stab wound to the chest.

Investigators suspect he may have met his killer on the street and brought him home. Mr. Carlos is the adopted son of the late Carlos film stars from the 1930s, the married Spanish acting duo who starred in classics such as "Tropicana Baby" and "Mambo Mamba."

An exhibition of Mr. Carlos' architectural design is being displayed for a limited time at the Museum of Modern Art located at 11 West 53rd Street.

Police are asking for any witnesses or leads to step forward.

SIX

Juan Carlos didn't have any surviving family, which is why his employees at Carlos Architectural Design felt obligated to handle the funeral services for him. Despite its reputation for being a seedy neighborhood, the workers decided to make arrangements at the Chinese-run Boe Fook Funeral Service on Canal Street because Juan loved the Lower East Side, or so says the newspaper in the obits. It also announces that his wake will commence tonight beginning at 6:30 p.m. I've decided to go.

Boe Fook is on Canal Street between Orchard and Ludlow, nestled between a Japanese hair salon and an acupuncture clinic that claims to cure everything from the nausea of pregnancy to cocaine abuse. Since I live on Orchard between Canal and Hester, it'll literally take me thirty seconds to walk to the wake. I take my time in the bathroom getting ready. Gelly is in the dirty kitchen right outside the bathroom. She chucks her Budget Gourmet dinner into the moldy microwave and gives the numbered panel Mike Tyson punches, selecting the cooking time for her frugal meal. I know she's angry because I've been in the bathroom for over an hour, but the way I look at it is I'm doing the bathroom a favor.

Holding a bunch of dirty laundry in my left arm, I exit the bathroom. She's leaning over the counter, shoveling forkfuls of runny sausage lasagna into her mouth. A droplet of tomato sauce is travelling down the corner of it. She breathes heavily through her nostrils.

"Took ya bloody long enough."

"Sorry Gelly, I have a wake to attend tonight."

"Who's it for?" she asks without making an effort of even sounding concerned.

"An acquaintance. No one I'm close to."

Juan Carlos is sitting in his beautiful bed, propped up by two large pillows covered in gold satin. He's wearing one of his signature white suits, with the duvet covering his body up to just before the shoulders. The morgue beautician has sculpted his facial expression into a tiny smile. He looks like he's having a wet dream about "Daddy's little boy." The rest of the funeral parlor has been crafted into a 1920s bedroom setting almost identical to his stylish penthouse.

The new fad in Manhattan is having a wake custom-designed to exhibit the deceased in his or her natural environment. The concept is called RESTyling.

The attendees at Juan Carlos' wake don't seem to notice me. A kneeling post has been placed in front of his bed. It's been crafted from a cushioned recliner. I lower myself, clasp my hands and close my eyes. I don't pray but instead struggle to remember what happened the night I murdered him.

I gain consciousness as I feel warm, thick liquid trickling down the middle of my forehead, taking a left down the side of my nose and continuing to my chin, off of which it drips. I let out a moan of pain and nausea and open my eyes. Trying to wipe the blood off my face, I discover that both my hands are tied with twine to either ends of the bed. I'm naked, sitting on the floor with my back against the end of the bed. A glass beer bottle with a chipped spout is lying on a tarnished silver tray next to me, along with a pair of sharp-looking scissors, a bowling ball pin and pliers. I hear humming and the sound of running water coming from the bathroom. Juan enters with latex-gloved hands raised, like a doctor about to perform surgery. A devilish grin is plastered across his face.

"Did baby boy get his rest?"

"Untie me, you fucking freak."

"Oh, I don't think cursing will help you, son, especially since I'm about to punish you for swearing at the teacher." The pitch in his voice is higher, as if he's talking to a child.

"Look, I don't need any money. Just let me go, please."

He walks to my left side and retrieves a wad of twine from the back pocket of his pants as he kneels. He lifts a thick steel post from the flooring and ties my leg to it. He then walks around to my right and repeats the process. If I try hard enough, I know I can free my legs from this, but I'm scared of what he might do in retaliation.

"We're just going to play a little game, my boy." He licks his lips. "My boy."

"Sir, please! No! Help! Someone please!" I scream as loud as I can.

He gently covers my mouth with his dry hand as his voice soothes, "No one can hear you. The only thing that yelling will do is annoy me. And trust me, you don't want to be in any more trouble than you already are. I took a broomstick with studded rusty nails to the last boy who disobeyed me. Now, do yourself a favor," he smiles sweetly, "And shut the fuck up!"

I close my eyes and my mouth, whimpering in defeat.

His hands bounce up and down through the air over his tools as he muses to himself, "Which one should I start with? Eeeny meeny minee moe!" His hand stops at the beer bottle. He picks it up and aims it at my crotch. "You like to get fucked, blueberry?"

"No, no please," I beg as I try to inch my buttocks away, but the twine tied to my limbs keeps them wide open. He holds me steady with ease as he jams the bottle into my ass. I feel the chipped glass scrape against my anus. He masturbates with his left hand while his right hand fucks me with the bottle.

In a violently euphoric rage, he orders me, "Say you're sorry, snookums! Apologize to the big baddie with a broken beer bottle! Oh, yeah!"

The flowers printed on the carpet are rotting. The roses are turning black. Weeds are choking the luscious landscape, and the caterpillars are coming to eat whatever is left. I pass out again.

SEVEN

Don't ask me why your kitchen is moldy when you sponge-paint your cabinets with a slice of bread, says my brain, thinking it's reciting the first lines of a brilliant new poem, as I fall asleep on the dish chair in my first Manhattan apartment on East 34th Street. Gelly gave two week's notice after Juan Carlos' service, and I had to find a place fast, not to mention a fast place to banish the few morbid memories of him that I've recovered.

Eyes open. I blink until they're moist enough to take in the ceiling above me. I'm staring at the shitty paint job. This apartment has been given the standard, cheap paint-over with each new tenant that has moved in and out of it for years. There must be ten coats of paint, one layer on top of the other. It reminds me of my father's mother, who slathered makeup on her face and soaked her gray hair in black dye. No matter how hard she tried, her hair always came out purple, and her concealer got lost in the wrinkles of her face. She can't paint over her old age and her ugly insides. I'm staring at my deceitful ceiling, and it looks cheap and desperate.

I settle on a peanut butter and jelly sandwich for breakfast. I don't keep much food in the house, partly because I'm never home, but mainly because I can't cook for shit. I flick on the TV and catch the second half of *Don't Tell Mom the Babysitter's Dead*. As bad as this old movie is, I've always appreciated Christina Applegate's ability to transform herself from a disgruntled teenager into a career woman. I watch, chewing with my mouth open, which makes me think of my grandfather, my mother's father, the only real grandparent I had.

When he was alive, he'd visit my mom's house every other day. She'd always have a plate of leftovers from the night before for him to take home. He'd sit at the dining room table and sip the coffee she'd put out and eat a pastry or doughnut. And he always chewed with his mouth open. I like to think that it's something he passed down to me.

He never did much with his life. He grew up on a farm and didn't make it past the sixth grade. He married late in his life, his wife died young, and he spent the rest of his years bowling, playing the lotto, and visiting his daughter every other day. I guess he was lonely. Maybe he passed that down to me, too.

New York is an abrupt place to live. Someone's always in your way or telling you to fuck off. The lines are always long. The people are always angry, sad or busy. Deal with it. Keep up or get out. Sink or swim. It's a constant struggle to survive whether it is financial, emotional or physical.

A large crowd is gathered around Joan Rivers in the middle of Grand Central Terminal as she does a bit for an upcoming show on the E! Network. I only catch a glimpse of her as I speed by, stealing peeks through the spaces between the arms and legs of tourists and rubberneckers. Her face is an off-white Halloween mask, clinging to the head by taut skin pulled behind her ears and tied into knots the size of bubblegum balls.

I climb the busy escalators, weaving through the crowds as I make my way into the MetLife building to begin another zombie-like day of work in the corporate world.

Sometimes I feel like waking up is such a waste of time. Putting on this suit and suffocating myself with this corporate tie. Sitting behind a desk and answering call after call. Transferring and holding and releasing and redialing and ringing and ringing and ringing! I think of Sean in prison and wonder if this is what he's going through. I understand the way time tortures someone, the way we submit to the way things are. I sit here for eight hours and think of nothing but freedom.

Lunch time. Whenever I spot two men of dramatically varying ages walking down the street, I can always decipher whether or not they're father and son. Like the idea that if you want to know what you're boyfriend will look like when he gets older, just look at his father. In many cases, this theory holds true. If you're feeling bored on a random day in the future, take time to compare and contrast a few pairs you might find in almost any location nationwide. Analyze the hairlines, their noses, or the similar expressions in each pair of eyes. Have pity on the sons whose fathers are balding, flabby, unattractive specimens. Love the beautiful ones. Be the fortuneteller of their physical future. Notice the closeness of their walk. Are they happy? I know when a son hates his father by the language of his body.

Sitting on a dark green folding chair in Bryant Park, I squander the last twenty minutes of my lunch break playing Father/Son I-Spy. A blond pair stroll by, their hair illuminated by streaks of brilliant sunlight, shaped by the sporadic holes between the leaves on the trees. The father is a few inches shorter than the tall son. They both wear khaki pants. The father has on a long-sleeved buttoned-down shirt, the son a white Polo shirt. The dad's hairline begins in the middle of the top of his head while the son sports longish hair, which begins at the top of his forehead. The pair doesn't speak as they walk, but there's a likeness in their stride. As they pass me in their silent exercise, I sense nothing but contentment.

I follow their lead and decide to begin the short walk back to work. The sky is open and blue. Gazing above the noisy traffic of people and cars, I experience a brief moment of tranquility. Suddenly, I hear a sound overhead. A commercial plane is flying low across Manhattan, so near to the ground that I can make out the name of the airline logo across the side of it: United Airlines. I lose sight of the plane as it flies past the buildings on 42nd Street, grateful that it wasn't a repeat September 11.

After work, I sit on the shuttle train and wait for its departure toward Times Square. I see an old man sitting diagonally across from me. He looks tired, as if he's waiting to die. I can't help but notice similarities between us, the pronounced bone structure, withered away by time and sagging skin. This happens to me often when I ride the subway. Sometimes I wonder if these old men are me from the future, traveled back in time to give me a glimpse of what's in store for me. I see the old man's liver spots, the hairy ears, and bald head with sporadic white sprouts of hair. I see his Salvation Army outfit, the emaciated body, the cane. I see wrinkle after wrinkle surrounding his lifeless eyes. No matter how bad things are, they can always get worse.

Evening. I'm now at a birthday party in a restaurant called Art Bar on 8th Avenue. Sitting in the middle of a crowd of familiar faces, I feel like a prisoner. A man wearing a buttoned-down shirt that looks as if it was made from an American flag gets up from his table and leaves with friends. All I can think of is how freedom has left me behind to sulk in the loneliness of well-known company.

There are levels of madness. It's also easy to substitute sanity with clothes, clean houses, friends, music, art. There are masks we wear to fool ourselves into believing we are like everybody else. But we're not. I watch myself laughing with friends. This is how I let these people see me.

I eat nachos and curly fries in the corner of the room as I sip a lukewarm glass of Pinot Grigio and listen to the faint sound of "Creep" sung by Radiohead, whispering from a speaker hanging on the wall above us. Spacing out from the music, I drop a nacho on an acquaintance's pant leg, and then apologize profusely.

It's nearing midnight and it's time to go home. I give shallow kisses and hugs to these strangers. Outside the rain pounds the hot pavement like tribal drums. Fifteen minutes later, I finally flag down a cab. I hop in the car, dripping wet.

It's 12:30 a.m. I'm lying on my twin-size loft bed from Ikea. Finally, my thoughts are not making any sense, which means I'm falling asleep. The ringing phone interrupts, and grumpy, I pick up.

"Hello?"

A sing-song robotic voice says, "This call is from a federal prison.

You will not be charged for this call. This call is from 'Sean.' Hang up to decline the call. Or to accept the call, dial five now."

"What's up, Sean?!"

"Hey, gurl, hey," he says.

He and I begin our usual conversation of how've you been, what's new, how's jail, how's New York, blah, blah, blah. Then he starts in with one of his stories. He asks if I remember Pineapple, and I do. He's that five-foot-tall Filipino from Arkansas who sells crystal—the first one to give it to me, too. We both used to hang out with him, and Sean even lived with him in Los Angeles for a few months while he was still running from the police. Pineapple was a nice enough person even though he sold and smoked a ton of crystal.

"Bitch, why did Pineapple call up Topher and tell him that his T-cell count is under a hundred or some shit?" He pauses briefly and then blurts out, "That freak has AIDS!"

There's a moment of silence, maybe two seconds. Then almost simultaneously we both crack up laughing. Five minutes pass and we still are. I haven't laughed so hard in so long. I don't even know what's so funny. After the phoniness of earlier this evening, the ultimate perversion of laughing about a mutual friend being HIV-positive is somehow liberating. Poor Pineapple. Sean's phone calls always leave me grinning.

EIGHT

I wish I could say I haven't become a prostitute but I can't. They say that only the one who hurts you can take the pain away, and maybe that's why I do this—well, that and probably the money, too. I don't know. I guess I'm just an ultramodern version of the American gigolo.

I have an ad posted on rentboy.com where I market myself as an All American white boy who's available for normal, safe, clean fun. I have an oral sex-only policy, I provide outcalls to Manhattan residents and offer a twenty-five-dollar discount to tricks who come to my place.

I screen potential hookups through a brief phone call. Listening to their voice, I pay close attention to the content of the conversation. If they ask too many obvious questions like, "How much for a blowjob?" or "What do I get for my two hundred bucks?" then I automatically assume it's a cop, though most likely they're just dumb. If they ask, "Do you get into anything else?" or "Do you like water sports?" then I immediately conclude they're a freak. I prefer to work with the nervous, deprived husbands who are in desperate need of a thrill, and the curious businessmen who haven't the time to shit let alone get laid. Those are my best customers, and they have good hearts, in spite of the rest of it.

White and dark laundry, clothes shopping, new hairstyle ideas and plans for the weekend are just a few of the things I concentrate on when a trick is sucking my cock. Sometimes I imagine it's Cale's shoulders I'm massaging, but most of the time I concentrate on daily inane tasks that I'll be able to get done once paid with the money necessary to perform them. It's not that it doesn't feel good; I can enjoy the orgasms if I let myself. It's not like I ever felt guilty or dirty about it. I'm numb to it. I'll get home, brush my teeth, take a shower and allow my lack of short-term memory to completely erase the act from my mind. All that's left is an outfit, a cocktail, an entree, rent. The only thing that makes me sad is the fact that I feel nothing, and even that's hard to feel since I feel nothing.

Since Juan Carlos attacked me, all I've wanted was a scent of an emotion, something to ride me through the hours, be it positive or negative. All I smell are sour balls, money and greed.

Human beings are victims of the weather. It's Sunday afternoon in the middle of July, and I'm in a cab that's tiptoeing to Penn Station. I ask the Jamaican driver to take the quickest route possible or I'm going to miss my train. I'm convinced he's decided to take extra time because I've requested it too rudely. The temperature is close to ninety degrees, and the air-conditioning in the cab barely works. The cool air that does blow from the tiny vents is laced with the stench of some foul lunch the cabbie must have enjoyed not long ago. Plus the taxi is a mini-van without windows that open. I make my train at the very last minute to New Hyde Park, a Long Island town thirty minutes outside the city.

He's waiting in the parking lot of the station in a dated corn-blue Crown Victoria. Halfway to the car I zone out and switch on a smile. I get in and greet Larry. He's a big guy, Jewish, late fifties, maybe six-two, at least 250 pounds, with a beer belly and a grey-haired buzz cut. His wooden cane rests on the seat. Larry mouths an uncomfortable hello. The tip of a nervous tongue darts out for a moment to touch a dry lip. He throws a nervous glance at me and then concentrates on the road for the ride back to his brick house, carrying on a casual conversation, neither of us putting much effort into it.

Later, I'm freezing in my underwear as I lie in an awkward position on his king-size bed. The rest of the house is warm, the windows are open, and summer is breathing into the house, but in the master bedroom Larry likes it cold. The bedroom is decorated with pictures of his wife and daughter. A 1970s wedding photo sits on a bureau. The wife has a strange fascination with *ET*, Larry tells me. There are dolls, posters and figurines of the famous creature sitting and hanging throughout the room.

I don't mind the visit so much this time since I know what to expect. I follow his commands given via gestures and passive aggressive comments that I easily catch. I do what I have to do. He tells me I'm gorgeous, how I'm the type of person someone could easily fall in love with. He asks me if I think he's a good kisser. I lie and tell him that he is, that he has nice lips. The truth is I feel like I'm being eaten by Audrey II in *Little Shop of Horrors*. His big saliva-dripping lips cut off my air supply and leave behind a slimy Marlboro residue from his smoking habit.

I'm not a victim. I'm aware of this as I try to imagine any hot guy I've slept with while Larry sucks my dick. He jolts me out of my meditation every time he scrapes my penis with his teeth, or possibly dentures. In the middle of break time—he likes to take his time, get his money's worth—his wife calls. She called the last time we did this, too. She's away on vacation with family while his eighteen-year-old daughter studies abroad in China. I lie there silent. How coincidental for her to call both times I've been here. What a message that should be to Larry, but he isn't paying attention to signs. He's concentrating on my lips on his neck. My fingers trace the scar that begins at the nape and travels a few inches past the shoulders. He tells me he had surgery because of cancer, which is why he has a cane and walks with a limp.

He swallows my cum. Now it's his turn. I put a condom on his three-inch penis and jerk it a couple of times. In less than sixty seconds he erupts. My lips haven't even touched the latex. I do him the favor of removing and flushing the condom, then return to him as he's putting back on his boxers. As I dress, he goes to a dresser drawer, pulls out three hundred bucks and lays it on the bed. Not bad for forty-five minutes of work, although last time he paid me six hundred bucks for my trouble. I cut him a deal this time, not because I want to be nice but because I'm desperate for cash.

"So what are your plans for the rest of the night?" I ask.

"Not sure," Larry replies. "I'd planned on stopping by a friend's barbecue, but to be honest I'm kind of worried about them smelling you on me."

I chuckle. "You serious, man? Just wash your hands and brush your teeth. You'll be fine."

"Yeah…" He looks guiltily out the driver-side window.

We drive back to the train station and carry on a casual conversation, neither of us putting much effort into it. We shake hands. Larry goes to eat, and I go home to Manhattan.

NINE

There is a definite difference between tricks and dates. I consider a trick to be company in exchange for money and a date to be company in exchange for pleasure. As I've gotten older, I've been using drugs less often, and have crossed over to promiscuous sex with strangers. I place ads on Craigslist each week, searching to orally pleasure straight males in my efficiency apartment. I like to call it "make-up sex." I make up for the ugly sex with my older sponsors by playing the submissive role in oral sex with pseudo-hetero strangers.

"Christian wants to die. Christian wants to die." These are the thoughts that run through my head during sex.

Beautiful, pseudo-hetero Brad text messages me: "Thanks man. That was hot!"

And I text message him: "U were hot! Call me if u wanna meet up again –Christian"

And he text messages me: "I definitely will. I am still hard thinking about you. –Brad"

Brad was hot. So was sucking his cock. He said he was about to cum and wanted to know where.

"In my mouth," I replied.

He exploded into my mouth. I ran over to my kitchen sink and acted as if I was spitting it out so as not to appear too slutty, as if meeting randoms from the Internet and sucking their cocks doesn't supersede the term "slutty" regardless of where they orgasm. I swallowed.

This wouldn't have been half as bad had I not had another Spanish date only an hour before. I took a quick cab down to 17th and 3rd. This guy was hot, too, but not as hot as Beautiful Brad. He left his apartment door open because he wanted me to walk in and start blowing him while he pretended to be asleep. Since he considered himself straight, he felt more comfortable getting a blowjob this way as opposed to acknowledging conscious homosexuality. With or without his eyes closed, he knew what I was doing. I played along because it was fun. And when he came in my mouth, I swallowed and went home.

When I got home, I went back online for an hour until I found Beautiful Brad. He just left twenty minutes ago. After he did and after I jerked off and came, that sentence started running through my brain.

"Christian wants to die. Christian wants to die."

Last night I sucked Dave's dick, a regular make-up sex of mine, because earlier yesterday I had pulled that trick Larry. That's four dicks in two days.

TEN

Joseph collects hundreds of different types of orchids. After our forty-five-minute session of oral sex in his Battery Park City duplex, he takes me on a tour upstairs. As he explains to me, Ophrys orchids have been regarded as an aphrodisiac and have been one of the main ingredients in certain love potions. I wonder if they'd help me enjoy myself more when he blows me. Looking at his unshapely body, I'd have to say probably not. He'll never be my type.

Joseph is a forty-something IT executive at a major pharmaceutical manufacturer and the longest running trick I have. Short, stout and Italian, he has dark brown hair and eyes. We keep it simple. We discuss politics, the arts, his frequent business trips to countries I've barely heard of and, of course, his orchids.

Using artificial lighting, he's turned his den into a greenhouse. It's warm and humid in the room, the perfect environment for most of his flowery friends. Those that require cooler temperatures are kept in large, climate-controlled cases the size of refrigerators. There are heat lamps and fans and sprays all doing their jobs automatically. The room is vented with flowing, filtered oxygen. Ivy traces the walls and ceiling.

He points out the recent blooms as he takes me down the rows of plants. He states their complicated names as if he were introducing me to his children. For a moment, I forget I'm the whore and pretend I'm the son, perhaps a young scientist-to-be being shown around his father's lab.

"This one is Phalaenopsis, or the moth orchid." He smiles at the flower and talks in a high-pitched voice. "And we have Cymbidium, and Paphiopedilum, otherwise known as lady slippers." His stubby hand cups the purple oddity with delicacy. They remind me of genital organs. The feeling of being a whore comes back.

"Here in the cooler we have Dendrobium. Down this row there's Oncidium and Vanda and…" He continues on with his show and tell. The heavy atmosphere is inviting, but the overload of sensuality is making me uncomfortable.

"I've got to get going soon," I mumble.

Joseph nods in acknowledgement but continues the tour.

After two more rounds of the room, I tell him I really need to go.

"Sure." He squeezes my ass one last time. So much for my orchid lesson.

He escorts me to the elevator and then the lobby, the gentleman that he is. We shake hands for show in front of the luxury building's personnel. He slides a couple hundred-dollar bills into my hand as it separates from his.

ELEVEN

It's 4 a.m. on a Saturday morning. I'm sitting on a mattress in the living room of a spacious, three-bedroom apartment located in the Financial District of Manhattan. My acquaintance, Nick, lives here along with two other lawyers. I've hung out with him for a while now. We met online. I was looking for drugs and sex. He had drugs. We see each other every couple of months, not to fuck but to poison our bodies. He recently moved to this new place and has yet to receive his furniture, hence the mattress-couch.

To ease the stress of my rough week, I had decided to have a glass of wine after work. One turned into two. Two turned into three. Three turned into, "I need to get some coke." I'd posted an ad on Craigslist, but instead of saying I was looking for pseudo-straight men, I advertised an interest in skiing, which is slang for doing blow. In no time I'd found a dealer. I purchased a gram of cocaine and an ecstasy pill.

When I got home, I felt guilty about wasting money on drugs, but luck was looking down upon my buyer's remorse. A fireman called to set up an appointment. He came over, I sucked his dick, easy money. He even gave me a fifty-dollar tip. After being reimbursed for my illegal purchases, I felt better about shoving line after line up my nose. I wasted most of the evening getting high by myself, listening to indie-rock and writing bad poetry. Nick text messaged me around midnight, inviting me over to party. I accepted and sped down in a cab.

He hands me the ceramic plate piled high with coke. I split my E with him. We're starting to feel the intoxication. After another white rail, he returns to his computer to chat with random men who are also up at this hour. Time races by in fast motion. My mumbling turns into a vibrating chatter. I'm having conversations about my personal history with myself. I think I'm talking to Nick, but I'm not. He's online, using my photo to lure two pseudo-straight muscle men over to chill, one of whom we think is hot. Only one has a picture, but Nick invites them, anyway.

The phone rings. Nick argues with me to answer it. When I do, I hear a deep voice.

"Christian?"

With hesitation I reply, "Yeah?"

"What's up man? This is Mark."

"Hey."

"What's goin' on?" I hear him blow a line.

"Not much," I say, despite the fact that everything is going on inside my body.

"You want us to come over?"

With a shaky voice, I give him the address that Nick passes onto me in sketchy whispers. The conversation ends. I immediately start freaking out.

"I can't do this, Nick. I'm just not together right now. I look scary."

He tries to console me. "Dude, you're f-fine. Don't worry."

We scramble around the apartment like a couple of cockroaches looking for a crevice or a drain to escape from the approaching humans. He gives me a toothbrush because I insist my breath stinks. He also lends me a pink and green striped Le Tigre polo, which I wear for twenty minutes before deciding the bright colors make my skin look like a mushroom. I resort back to my black T-shirt that has armpit stains and not so pleasant odors emanating from it. We hide the drugs because, until these guys lay out their own provisions, we don't want to take any chances on them being possible coke fiends. Then we unhide the drugs because we forgot we want to do a line. We hide them again. It's 5:45 a.m.

Fifteen minutes have passed, and we're doing another line from the drugs we again unhide. It took us five minutes to find them because we couldn't remember where we put them due to the multiple times they were relocated. At 6:05 a.m. Nick starts stressing.

"They're not coming," he declares, his foot tapping the glass coffee table.

"Yes, they are. It *does* take more than five minutes to get down here, Nick. There aren't that many people who live in Manhattan who have ever even been to this part of it." I chew my gum as if my jaw is running a mouth marathon.

"No, they're not. They have my address. What if they're cops?"

"They probably aren't."

"But what if they are?"

"They're not, Nick, relax…What if they're like serial killers?"

He freezes in deep, dark thought. "I'm hiding the kitchen knives."

"I don't care if they are, just as long as they shoot me instantly. I just don't want to feel any pain like those freaky ones who like to cut people up with machetes."

"What the fuck are you talking about?" he implores as he chucks all sharp kitchen utensils, scissors and fine-tip ballpoint pens into the oven. Without warning, the doorman downstairs calls to tell Nick his guests have arrived. In a shaky voice he utters, "Send them up."

I take a big gulp of saliva as I try to adjust my greasy, unmanageable hair with my trembling, coke-caked fingers.

He heads for the door. "Come on."

My head twists shakily left to right. "This was your idea. This is your house. You answer it."

"Come on, man! It's your picture they saw."

"Ugh. Fine." I stop in the bathroom for one last desperate mirror-glance. First, we each check the peephole for glimpses of our dates, but we're too fucked up to see anything, so we open the door a smidge. We peek out of the tiny crack as two scared children hiding in the closet from the Boogey Man. The two men are strutting cockily down the hallway. When the duo is close enough to see the glint of our eyes coming from the dark apartment, Nick swings the door wide open to greet them. As I examine them quickly, Nick shows them in.

Mark is around six-two with slightly receding black hair, wearing eyeglasses and he has a thin, toned frame. He wears a short-sleeved, buttoned-down red plaid shirt and dark True Religion corduroys. Alex is slightly shorter. He takes off his hat to reveal longish blond hair. His eyes are dark blue. He's wearing army greenish cargo pants and a gray T-shirt. His body is sturdier, a bit more masculine than Mark's.

I lead the way into the living room where I resume my knees-to-chest sitting position on the mattress-couch. Alex helps himself to the restroom. He pees with the door open while Mark sits next to me, looking me over like a fat man does to his food. The credits of the teenybopper film, *Bring It On*, are rolling on the twenty-seven-inch TV screen in front of us. Alex comes out of the bathroom, adjusting his dick and zipping his pants in transit.

We sit in silence for a few minutes until Nick retrieves the plate of coke. Each of us blows a couple of lines, and then we sit in silence again for a few more minutes. I attempt to spark a conversation.

"So what do you guys do?"

Mark looks hazy. "Huh?"

"Do. What do you guys do for work?"

Mark speaks first. "Well, I'm a real estate developer."

Alex chimes in. "And I'm a personal assistant."

"For a celebrity?"

"No, just someone who's really, really rich," he explains.

"Oh, okay."

Mark asks, "And you?"

"I write mostly. And Nick is a lawyer."

Each of us acknowledges the other's careers, and then we sit in silence again for a few more minutes. Alex breaks the second layer of ice. "Got any porn?"

Nick stammers, "N-No but there's always P-Pay-per-view."

Alex rubs his hands together, "Oh, yeah."

I feel my insides grumble. I'm uncomfortable and sketchy as it is. In no way will straight pornography ease my anxiety. I don't even know why these men are here. I will not be engaging in an orgy.

Alex selects *Cumsicle*. The television screen is immediately bombarded with straight sex. Under the opening credits, six men ejaculate into a woman's mouth. She then spits into an ice tray and sticks a toothpick into each plastic cubicle. In the next scene, she unveils her frozen creation. The video now treats us to a flashback, showing in detail how the material used in the manufacturing of cumsicles was encouraged to appear. No one says a word.

Unexpectedly I speak. "What the fuck are we doing?"

We all start laughing at how ridiculous this is, us meeting at six in the morning. As my giggles subside, I glance at Mark, making unplanned eye contact. This prompts him to take the liberty of placing his right foot on top of mine. My body instantly tenses even more. Alex has reached behind Mark's back and is massaging the nape of my neck. I look at Nick whose leg is now interlocked with Alex's, his hand massaging Alex's crotch. Alex's right leg is knit into Mark's left, with his hand massaging his crotch. I sustain the knees-to-chest sitting position, my face contorted into an uncomfortable expression as I attempt to ignore the molestation. I feign focus on "Cintia," the porn star enjoying her creamy frozen dessert, but to no avail.

My anxiety builds as my drug high climaxes. Scared and nervous, I peer at Nick again. My eyes, blurred by the ecstasy, take a few seconds to adjust to the four-foot distance between us. When they clear, instead of Nick I see Andrew, my dead brother. I squint to make out his face. His head, now attached to Nick's body, is glaring at me disapprovingly. His form ripples like a still body of water when the surface is troubled. He's still sixteen, even though by now he'd be two years older than I am. His face disappears as the ripples cease and my head calms. Overcome with awe, I stare at Nick, transfixed. He looks at me questioningly.

"Christian, are you okay?"

The two pseudo-straights turn their heads to me.

I break my statue pose and leap to my feet. "I have to go."

Mark protests. "What? You can't leave, man. We just got here."

"I know, but I f-feel retarded."

Alex perks up. "We all do, man. Come on. Try to relax."

"No, that's okay. I'll relax when I get home."

Alex hops off the mattress-couch and begins massaging my shoulders while Mark stays seated, obviously frustrated. Cintia fakes a moan to demonstrate how delicious her cold treat is.

Mark tries another tactic. "Do some more coke, man."

"I don't think so."

Trying to mask his irritation, Alex whispers in my ear, "But you dragged us all the way out here, dude."

Resentful of his expectations I say, "Yeah to chill. I didn't promise anything."

Mark sighs with frustration and continues to look at the porn. My back to the TV, I watch Cintia's escapades continue in the reflection of his glasses while I zone out of Alex's fondling. Nick goes to the bathroom. Mark stands and walks to me, presses his body against mine, starts kissing my neck. I feel Alex's hands lifting the back of my T-shirt. He briefly massages my lower back, and then, without warning, his hands dive down the back of my jeans.

"I feel weird. I can't do this."

"Yes, you can," Mark insists.

I want to break the bones in their dirty, demanding hands. "Get off m-me."

"Ssshh." Alex pulls his hands out of my pants and wraps his arms around my waist. He drags me backward into Nick's bedroom while Mark pushes from the front. I open my mouth but no words come out. I try to fight them off, but my physical strength has been robbed by the drugs. Alex throws me on the bed while glancing at Mark knowingly. "Lock the door."

Mark turns the switch on the knob with his left hand while he unzips his pants with his right, his mouth contorting into a Joker grin.

Alex looks at me, disgusted. "No little pretty boy faggot is gonna play fucking games with us. Now take off your fucking pants." The image of Juan Carlos' face flashes across Alex's like the demons in the film, *The Devil's Advocate*.

"No."

Mark speaks up. "Dude, you can either be willing to have a good time with us, or we'll make you. I recommend willing. Suck my dick." He pulls down his pants and shoves his erect penis in my face.

Alex joins in on the assault, "That's right man, and you better suck his good or else I'll make it hurt when I'm fucking you."

I cringe. I'd once fantasized about being raped by two hot straight men, but now that it's actually happening, I realize it's not what I want. It just reminds me of Juan Carlos. Where's Nick?

The anger in Mark's voice rises. "I'm gonna count to five, and you better be choking on my cock by then or else—"

Suddenly, there's a violent rapping on the door. "Hello? What's going on in there?"

His eyes unwavering from mine, Mark pulls up and zips his pants. "Everything's fine, man." He struts over to the door.

Alex, standing on the bed, bends down and quietly says, "If you know what's good for you, you won't say a word about this to your buddy."

Mark turns the lock. Nick instantaneously swings open the door. Sweat oozes out my pores as if I've had a high fever that just broke.

"What are you guys doing?" Nick looks to me for some sign. I return the look yearningly, wanting to cry for help even though I'm no longer in danger. With three sets of eyes on me, I scan the room for my gray and bright blue sneakers. I spot them in the corner, underneath a pair of boxers that have fallen out of Nick's overstuffed laundry basket.

"You leaving, man?" Mark's voice has returned to its faux innocence.

"Y-yeah, I have to get to bed. I have plans tonight, and I need to rest."

"Hey, well, it was really nice to meet you. Hope we can hang out again sometime." Alex's mouth molds into a dishonest smile as he extends a hand. Reluctantly, I oblige the gesture. Mark pats me on the back as I brush past him.

Nick walks me to the front door. "You sure you're okay? You're gonna get home safe, right?"

I wave him away. "Yeah, yeah."

In confidence, he whispers, "What was going on in there?"

My eyes slowly begin to well with tears. I pull out my designer sunglasses that Sean stole for me back in San Fran and get them on my face just before the first drop trickles from my eyes.

"Nothing."

I don't say goodbye. I just turn around and walk toward the elevator. On the way down, it suddenly occurs to me that I'm leaving my drug buddy with two potentially dangerous men. Is it that I don't really care about him? Or is it that I can't imagine anyone could be as powerless as I am? I say good morning to the security guard in the lobby who's just replaced the one on the midnight shift. The first car coming down the street is a cab. I flag it down, get in and ride home.

TWELVE

It's not how you feel. It's how you look. I'm reciting this over and over again in my head as blood literally gushes from my right nostril. I've run out of tissues and toilet paper, and I've been reduced to shoving a rough paper towel up my sore nostril to plug the outpour. After last night's debauchery of cocaine and attempted sexual assault by strangers, I'm surprised I don't feel worse.

It's a couple hours later, and Beautiful Brad stops over. We haven't hooked up in over a month, and it's good to see him. He waltzes in, his suit jacket hanging on his arm, his shirt unbuttoned halfway. In his other hand, he carries a duffle bag. He just came from the gym, all tight and showered. He flashes a cute smile the way a man does when he knows he's about to get laid, positions himself on my dish chair and I sit on the floor between his hard legs.

After fifteen minutes of sucking, I gaze upward into his eyes.

"Dude."

"Yeah?"

"I think your nose is bleeding."

I look down, and sure enough, blood is streaming into his pubic hair, mixing with my saliva. I jump up and bolt for the bathroom. Grabbing tissue after tissue, I attempt in vain to stop the eruption.

"I'm sorry, man. It's just that the air at the office I work in is really dry, and I've been getting nosebleeds because of it."

"It's cool. It happens."

My nose plugged with tissues, I glance at him through the bathroom door as he stares at his erect cock, waiting patiently.

Five minutes pass, and I'm still in the bathroom, keeping the blood from pouring out of my nose with my thumb and pointer finger. The sink and toilet are smeared with blood. Red drops litter the tiles on the floor. At this point I give up blowing Beautiful Brad. Even if I got the hemorrhaging to stop, it would only happen again once we started getting physical.

"Maybe you should go."

"You sure?"

"Yeah, I'm not really into it anymore. Plus, I know I wouldn't want some guy whose nose had just been bleeding to give me head."

As he pulls up his pants, he asks, "Yeah, you sure you're okay, though?"

My fingers pinching my nose shut, I tell him, "I'm fine. Thanks. Sorry."

"It's cool," he says as he exits.

At this moment, I want to die. How embarrassing! Didn't he even want to wash it off? I better admit why my nose was really bleeding since he's probably already assumed the truth. I send him a text message.

"I'm not gonna lie. I did coke last night, and my nose has been fucked up since then."

He text messages me back: "Figured."

"Hope you want to hang out again."

"Definitely. You're a great cocksucker and good-looking. Lay off the coke, man."

"Thanks. I'll talk to ya soon."

I breathe a sigh of relief but am still mortified.

THIRTEEN

George Smith is at least eighty-five years old. I reluctantly open the door to my apartment and am attacked by tidal waves of his overwhelming cologne. The first thing I notice about him is how neat he is. He's wearing dark beige corduroy pants with extra large ribbing and brown leather oxfords with tan socks. His crisp, white, buttoned-down shirt is covered by a snug, light gray cashmere sweater. He wears a heavy, black wool overcoat and a black cashmere scarf. He takes off a cocoa-colored hat adorned with a colorful peacock feather and holds it to his chest as his other hand reaches out to me with a bottle of red wine. I smile awkwardly as I let him in.

"Why don't we break open this wine and have ourselves a drink?" he suggests, and wastes no time making a feeble move on me after just a sip. The dried-up orifice on his face that used to be his mouth gently presses against my reluctant cheek. As sandpaper hands massage my left arm, I cringe but repeatedly say to myself, "Just think of the money!"

We're making out, and suddenly he's short of breath. I suggest we take a break. He goes for his glass of red wine and miscalculates, knocking the cup off the table; it crashes against the wall, staining it red. A memory of my encounter yesterday with Beautiful Bloodied Brad attacks my conscious. Trying to ignore it, I focus on cleaning the mess. I know the blot won't come off. The red will always remind me of these times of ill-work.

We resume our date. I'm sitting at the top of my twin loft bed, laughing hysterically inside as I watch George struggle to climb the ladder. In a way, I feel sorry for him. I vow to myself that I'll never be that horny.

After about two long minutes, he makes it to the top, panting and weak. The sweat from his exertion, combined with the stench of perfume, resonates in my nostrils and impregnates the sheets of my bed. I will smell it for days.

After more than fifteen minutes of rest and small talk, he's sitting on my chest, thrusting himself into my mouth in the slowest of motions. I keep bracing myself for him to have a heart attack and collapse on my chest.

Finished with my job, I now wait at the bottom of the loft bed ladder as requested by George. He tells me how he had his hip replaced six months ago, and he wants me to catch him if he falls as he climbs down. He doesn't fall. He gets dressed as quick as a snail, gives me a crusty kiss on the cheek, pays me and leaves.

FOURTEEN

After a day of monotonous office work, following a slow night of George, I meet up with Hartley, the married commercial real estate broker. He has thick black hair, a tan complexion and beady, dark eyes that hide behind rimless eyeglasses. Five-ten, he has a moderately hairy, slightly toned body. He's thirty-seven, the father of two girls, ages four and six. He lives and also conducts most of his business on Long Island, but on the infrequent occasions when he works in the city, he always text messages me for a date.

He drives a black, fully equipped, BMW Z4 Roadster, blasts trendy indie-rock music from his iPod, which is connected to the car stereo. When we spend time together, he addresses me as "dude" or "bro," using phrases like "chillin' out" and "sweet."

He texts me to let me know he's waiting outside my apartment. He enjoys the fantasy of us hanging out like two college kids. I walk to his car and sit in the deep, soft seat. The smoothness of the leather against my ass makes me feel like I'm hovering. We speed away, running a light that just turned red, and corner the block like a rollercoaster on rails. We glide down Second Avenue.

"What's up, bro? Haven't seen you in awhile, dude." He shakes my hand in fraternity fashion, slapping my palm, quick firm grip, and then a lingering tug as he pulls away.

From the corner of my eye I see him pick his nose swiftly. He pulls a booger from his left nostril and flicks it out the window, unaware of my disgusted observance. "Yeah, dude, I just had a business dinner at Mr. Chow's up on 57th. I only went 'cause I had Japanese clients visiting from London to check out some buildings in the city. They wanted to go to Chow's, I took 'em to Chow's, you know?"

The lights from the buildings, cars and streetlamps have become yellow and red lines, seamlessly connected by Hartley's manic driving.

"Eh...I had a few vodkas, oh and dude, you're not gonna believe this shit. Some motherfucker was sitting two tables away from me, guess who it was?"

"I give up," I reply without guessing.

"Fucking Mick Jagger, bro. 'Cept it wasn't Jagger. It was some crazy dude dressed up like Jagger. He got free drinks, free food and left with these hot-ass blond sluts. It was only after he left that the wait staff checked out a recent photo of Mick online, and it turned out this dude was a fraud."

"That's crazy."

"So where do you want to go?" He turns to me when he asks me this question and nearly runs over a pedestrian.

"Mr. Brightside," a popular song by The Killers, begins pumping from the car speakers.

"Dude, I fucking love this song. It's awesome!"

"Yeah, me too," I mutter.

He turns the music up even louder than it already is. He screams the lyrics with the windows rolled down. When we stop at traffic lights, I crouch down low in my seat.

We park in front of Dark Room on Ludlow. "This is it, buddy. Let's get some drinks. You want some blow? I got blow."

"I knew you were on something. You've been acting way too happy."

He laughs as if I just said the funniest thing in the world. "Dude, you're hilarious." He pulls a baggie from the back pocket of his black pants. He takes the key out of the ignition and scoops up a bump-size portion of the cocaine. "This is for you, my friend."

"I don't know."

"C'mon man, one little bump never hurt anybody," he whines.

"Alright, but just one. I don't want to be up all night."

"Thadda boy."

He lifts the key to my nose. I sniff. I remember the taste of the drip in the back of my throat, the rush. "Let's go get a drink."

I'm on my second vodka-tonic at Dark Room and starting to feel edgy. I believe the only two other people at the bar are staring at me. They're wearing clothes that want to be Lower East Side-trendy, but fail miserably. It's obvious they just moved here from Nebraska. The bartender is wearing all black. His lip and nose ring are out of place on a thirty-year-old face. The three of them continue to steal judgmental glances at me. Who are they to size me up? I may be a glorified prostitute, but at least I'm not making two-dollar tips at thirty or wearing frayed Gap jeans in an effort to be stylish.

"Can we get out of here?"

"Sure, dude. It's already eleven. I gotta be home by like 12:30ish or the wife'll start worrying."

We arrive at my apartment alive, much to my surprise, considering Hartley's obscene driving. As he's prepping to exit the vehicle, I'm snorting two additional bumps of coke. My hand trembles as I lift the key to my nostril. Despite the small quantity of the drug I've taken, I'm high. The thoughts in my brain are changing and collide with each beat of my heart.

Inside, he charges toward the bathroom and proceeds to pee for the champion title of longest pisser.

"I see you still got this Ikea loft bed," he states as he eyes the furniture from the bathroom.

"Yeah," I agree with faint despair.

He chuckles. "Dude, you've gotta figure something out." His behind jiggles as he shakes the final drips from his dick.

"I thought you of all people would appreciate a dorm-like setting," I joke.

"Huh?"

I snort. "Never mind."

He zips his pants and enters the living space. He notices a pile of my CDs and begins flipping through them. "Dude, I've been meaning to check out BRMC. Can you burn it for me?"

"Uh, sure," I say, although I really don't want to.

"I forget what that stands for."

"Black Rebel Motorcycle Club," I murmur disinterestedly.

"Ah, okay."

I check the time. It's 11:45.

"We should probably get to it. You're gonna be late coming home as it is."

"You're right," he agrees as he unzips his pants.

He's on top of me. His upper body is supported by two toned arms that are posted on either side of my head. Sweat is dripping from his forehead onto me. I feel the squishiness of the lube mixing with our limp genitals as his lower body presses against mine.

"We shouldn't have done so much coke."

"Yeah." He wipes his face with his left hand, shifting his weight to his right side.

I close my eyes. I just want this to end. I hear high-pitched wheezing sounds and open my eyes. "Hart, you sound congested. Want me to get you a tissue? Besides, I feel gross covered in lube."

"It isn't me."

"What?"

"It isn't me, the wheezing I mean. And anyway that's not wheezing, dude. It's more like squeaking." He climbs off me, releasing a disappointed sigh. We both lie silently for a moment until I hear it again.

"It's coming from below." I climb down.

The squeaking seems to be located underneath a rack of clothes. I weave through the metal furniture until I reach the source of the sound. A mouse is stuck by its head to a glue trap I laid under the rack weeks ago when I spotted one peeking out of my stovetop. It had gotten into the oven through the exhaust pipe coming from the drywall. Now, looking at my furry prisoner, I wonder if it's the same intruder or an identical counterpart.

It reminds me of a pair of Siberian dwarf hamsters I had as pets when I was young. I named them Andy and Chris. Andy was bigger than Chris. There was a plastic toy cottage that I kept in the cage with them. They'd always snip at each other. Being a distracted adolescent, I didn't notice Chris' absence until it was too late. Andy kept him captive in the little house for days, biting his paws if he tried to escape.

Hamsters are territorial rodents. Chris died of starvation. Andy overate after he murdered him, died of gluttony a couple months later. I buried them both in our front yard behind thick hedges.

I pick up the trap, mouse and all, and carry it over to the few square feet of open space I have in my apartment. I lay my head on its side and look into the opaque eyes of the terrified creature. He stops squirming.

I'm interrupted by the fatal, Herculean stomp of Hartley's suddenly shoed foot on the mouse. The mouse releases a final, shrill goodbye.

"What the fuck did you do?!" The pitch of my voice matches the mouse squeak.

Hartley lifts his foot, the bottom of his shoe oozing with mouse goo. "I'm doing you a favor, bro. You know how many germs those little fuckers carry?"

He picks up the trap with what's left of the pest and throws it into the grocery bag filled with garbage that I have hanging from my front doorknob. He reaches for the paper towels on top of the refrigerator.

"Get out!"

"What?"

I repeat: "Time's up, Hart. I want my money, and I want you to leave."

I close my eyes and let out a big sigh.

He stares intently at me with either anger or pity. After a moment that feels like forever, he dresses hurriedly, counts out two of the three hundred dollars he owes me for my time.

"I didn't cum. That's all you're getting."

I don't argue. He walks out the front door, leaving me with one last quizzical look as I lie dazed and naked on the hardwood floor amidst the rattrap, mice guts and twenty-dollar bills.

FIFTEEN

A ndrew White died when he was sixteen. It was Michelle's ninth birthday party. I was fourteen at the time. That morning, my brother was getting ready to go to a friend's house a few blocks away. I was pleading with him to let me come along, but he insisted I stay home. I always wanted to hang out with him and his friends. We argued constantly, got into fisticuffs regularly, and laughed together occasionally. We weren't the best of friends, but he was my brother. I loved him. Now that I'm older, I find life harder without him.

I wasted that day watching TV and playing Nintendo. At fourteen, there wasn't much else to do. During my flight as the princess in *Super Mario Bros. 2*, the phone rang. My sister was outside playing Barbie with friends on the driveway. My mother was out shopping for the party, and my stepfather was mowing the lawn. I picked up the receiver. It was my elementary school teacher, Mrs. Cardoza. She was calling to let us know that a teenage boy had been hit by a car in front of her house. She said that the face was unrecognizable and the boy had no identification on him. If we heard of anyone's family looking for their son, then we should tell them to contact Saint Vincent's Hospital. As best she could, she gave me a brief physical description of the boy. He had a small, gold hoop in his left ear. He wore a white sweater, blue jeans and white Nike sneakers. He'd been listening to a black walkman. I noted the information in my head but kept myself from thinking much of it.

Michelle's birthday party began around 7 p.m. Mom was irate because my brother hadn't come home; she'd specifically told him to be back by five. My stepfather didn't seem to be concerned about it. He was used to Mom's overreactions.

My step relatives had arrived, along with my grandfather, and my mother's friends. Michelle had invited two friends from school to sleep over. Mom had prepared veggies and dip, chips, wings, stuffed breads and her popular clam dip. Despite my brother's absence, everyone was having a good time.

Mom grew angrier as the night wore on. She'd waited for Drew to arrive to sing "Happy Birthday" to Michelle. When it was close to 10 p.m., the anger shifted to worry. She started to zone out, no longer participating in the party. My stepfather covered for her, keeping conversations going. As Mom stood by the kitchen window in a daze, her hands plunged in dirty dishwater, her friend Mary said, "Jean, hon, you okay?"

"Something's wrong."

Mary swallowed a mouthful of chewed carrots. "The food's great."

"Something happened to Andrew. I can feel it." Mom gazed out the window in a frozen trance.

My stepfather caught the remark and glanced at his wife with exasperated irony. "Jean, he's probably just lost track of time."

Mary nodded in agreement as she picked her teeth with her long, polished fingernail.

"He's been late before but not late like this. He wouldn't miss his sister's birthday," insisted Mom.

Suddenly I remembered Mrs. Cardoza's phone call. "Oh," I mentioned casually, "Miss Cardoza called a while ago..."

Mom's eyes widened. "Why in God's name didn't you tell me this before, Christian?!" A hush filled the room.

"I don't know."

Mom swung open the cabinet under the kitchen sink and dug through the cleaning products to find the phonebook buried beneath. She began calling hospitals, asking them if there was a boy admitted that had been hit by a car. My stepfather's party mood began to seriously wane. He came over to my mom and stood there, looking helpless, his arms dangling at his side. Bridgeport Hospital said no. Saint Michael's said no. Then I remembered Saint Vincent's and told Mom. A nurse informed her that an unidentified boy had been hit by a car and admitted into the hospital earlier that afternoon. Mom described my brother, including the pierced ear. The color drained from her face. The phone fell out of her hand and bounced on the floor. She ran to get her purse from her bedroom.

As she scrambled to find her car keys, she said, "He's been admitted into the hospital under the name John Doe."

"Mom, it may not be him—"

"Christian this is your fault." She pointed her finger at me like she was cracking a case of the board game *Clue*. "All day and you didn't say a thing. I could've helped him."

"I didn't know what to say."

"Go to your room! I can't even look at you!"

My eyes welled. I looked at my stepfather imploringly, his face turned away. With hunched shoulders, I shuffled to my room while she left the house, followed woodenly by my stepfather. My mother's friends and step relatives tried to console me. My mother was upset, she didn't know what she was saying. I didn't believe them. All I could think of was the possibility that my brother was hurt and that it was my fault because I'd known all day and hadn't said a thing. They brought me back to the living room. Next to Mary on the couch, I fell into a dazed sleep, my usual solution when I don't want to think about anything.

A gentle but firm hand shook my right arm. The first thing I saw was the time on the VCR: 2:09 a.m. The first thing I smelled was the leather of my stepfather's bomber jacket. The first thing I heard was my mother weeping. Mary must have left during my slumber. I sat up and saw my mother and stepfather clinging to each other like two lost children. Mrs. Cardoza was sitting on the loveseat adjacent to the couch. She must have come over to babysit after the others left. I looked into Mom's red eyes. I already knew the answer to the question

I was about to ask.

"Was it him?"

She nodded.

"Is he okay?" My voice was below a whisper. If she wasn't able to hear my question, then maybe her answer wouldn't be true.

She and my stepfather pulled me into their arms.

"He's dead, baby. Andrew's dead."

The boy I was died that night.

Andrew White was walking to his friend's house along Huntington Turnpike in Bridgeport, Connecticut when he was a struck by a car from behind. The driver sped away. It was called a hit and run. Witnesses thought they saw a red Camaro.

He was inflicted with severe head trauma. When he was taken to the hospital, the doctors raced to save his life by performing emergency brain surgery. It failed. He was pronounced brain dead. They kept his body on life support while they waited for permission from my mother to donate his organs. She had hesitantly agreed.

He was lying on the hospital bed, his head wrapped in bandages. His entire body was swollen like a balloon due to the preservation fluids to keep his organs alive. I did not recognize him. I was supposed to say goodbye, but I couldn't. I turned away, crying. Outside in the waiting room, Sister Michael, a nun from our parish, tried to console me by hugging me, but the attempt failed because the only thing I could concentrate on was her horrible breath. She asked me to try to imagine my brother as happy and quoted something from a scripture: "If you knew where I was going, you would gladly let me go." At the time it was comforting.

Almost all my brother's organs were donated. For several months after his death, we received morbid, anonymous letters, thanking our family for my brother's heart, kidneys, eyes, etc. It was awful.

The day before the wake, I was sitting on the front porch. Drew's classmate, Melissa, was walking by. She stopped to express her condolences for my family's loss and said that she'd seen Drew the day he died. He'd greeted her as she was taking out the trash. He was on his way to a friend's house, but before leaving, he stopped and turned toward her.

"Melissa, if I die, will you come to my funeral?"

"Of course, what kind of question is that?"

"Just wondering. See ya," he'd said, then continued his walk to doom.

The casket was closed for the wake because of the organ donations. I was worried about the wake. I didn't want to go because of my real father. My mother had heard he was being let out of prison for the day so he could pay his respects. Luckily, it was arranged so he would attend the wake prior to our arrival. When we got there, he'd already gone, but his was the first name that had been signed in the guest book. I could picture him scribbling it with his wrists shackled together. The truth was his penmanship was extremely neat. The cursive writing was large and flowery like a woman's. I signed my name below his. I didn't remember what he looked like, but I imagined his hands. I examined mine as I wrote and wondered if they were like his, praying they weren't.

There was a life insurance policy worth about forty thousand dollars in my brother's name. The only people who could access the money were his legal guardians. After the funeral, my father's lawyers were able to manipulate the law in order to take half of the money that was supposed to go toward me for school. He pleaded that his portion would be given to his ailing mother. Whether or not his argument was valid, my father didn't deserve any money involving the death of a boy he'd abandoned.

A sidewalk was built on Huntington Turnpike in my brother's name, after a neighborhood petition was presented to the city council. It detailed complaints of the many accidents that had occurred on that street. They called the new pavement Andrew White's Way. The police had no leads as to who'd killed my brother. But it didn't matter anyway because I already knew who did it. It was me.

After my brother died, my mother began attending mass every day, and would make me aware of every sin I committed. Her newfound religion, however, hadn't corrected her foul tongue. By calling me a faggot and a cocksucker, it was she who told me I was gay. I ran away from home junior year.

I lived for nine months as a transient, temporarily dwelling in the homes of generous ravers and attending all-night dance parties with them. Most of us were underage and on designer drugs. We spoke of peace, love, unity and respect. We'd travel across three states just to attend an event where a good DJ was spinning.

I was living in Torrington, Connecticut, at my friend Laura's home when I was arrested for "evading responsibility." She'd let me borrow her car while she went to work at a fancy restaurant. When I pulled out of the parking space, I scraped her car against a black Mercedes and drove off. The police pulled me over minutes later. Because I was sixteen, they called my mother.

I saw her in court for the first time in almost a year. She was down the hall, sitting alone with her hands on her lap, almost as freaked out as I was. We looked at each other, and both of us started crying.

Evading responsibility is considered a serious offense. Leaving the scene of an accident, regardless of the circumstances, is labeled as a hit and run. The Torrington courts looked at my crime as if I'd hit a human being and driven off. They wanted to put me in juvenile detention for one year. Being a runaway and a high school dropout didn't help matters. Mom convinced the judge I was a good kid and that I was going to move home, finish school and stay out of trouble. He fined me five hundred dollars with the condition that I'd be forced to serve the one-year jail sentence in addition to whatever penalty was assessed for the second crime if I were to get into any kind of trouble before my eighteenth birthday.

I spent the next couple of years walking on eggshells *with* my mother when I moved back home. We both tried to refrain from words or actions that would offend the other. I went to night school and earned my high school diploma with honors, and I worked as a cashier at a grocery store. She quit waiting tables and began working in an office as a bookkeeper. Michelle was in junior high.

When my stepfather was promoted to a managerial position at the silicon factory where he worked, we moved to a pale yellow, two-bedroom house in Trumbull, a safe suburb just outside of Bridgeport. Since there weren't enough bedrooms, I slept on the three-season back porch. My stepfather installed a heating vent and put bamboo blinds on the massive windows. At night the neighbors living in the house behind ours could see through the cracks. Sometimes I caught them spying on me. I began walking naked and prayed that the thirty-year-old male of the couple would climb down the steep hill, break in my bedroom and rape me. He never came.

My weekend endeavors evolved from raves into gay clubs such as Gotham Citi in New Haven. The admission was limited to people over twenty-one, but I always found a way in, either by sleeping with an employee or using a fake ID. Cocaine became my drug of choice. I'd stay up all night. On the drive home from whomever's house, my eyes would be glued to the rearview mirror as I was convinced that every car behind me was a cop.

When I'd get home, Mom would be up reading the newspaper, acting like nothing was wrong. I'd lie that I'd gotten drunk and fallen asleep at a friend's place. I'd tell her I was still tired and remain in bed all day and night, surfacing only to go to the bathroom or eat one of her home-cooked meals. She'd go to church twice on Sunday. During dinner, after we blessed the food as a family, she'd say a silent prayer for me, and I always knew it because I became accustomed to reading her lips, especially words like "Christian" and "cocksucker." I wondered which offended her god more, my behavior or her language. On Monday we'd both go to work and then repeat the weekly monotony of lies and introversion.

Her religious fanaticism worsened. Sometimes she "talked to God," but it just looked like she was schizophrenic and having conversations with herself. My stepfather stuck by her side as long as he could. He eventually moved out, leaving my mother for another woman who wasn't very attractive.

Strangely, my sister excelled in school while the melodrama continued. I guess it was her way of escaping the hell called family life. She went from being a C-student to getting straight A's and being on the honor roll. During her first semester as a freshman at Trumbull High School, she joined the cheerleading squad, girls' basketball team, and chess club.

The truce between my mother and I began to end. I stopped coming home early in the morning after partying because when I did she'd just berate me with insults. She'd say I deserved to burn to death like the degenerates of Sodom and Gomorrah. Sometimes I thought I did too, but I'd never admit it.

SIXTEEN

Michelle picks me up from the train station. I called her last night to tell her I was coming in, that I needed to visit Saint Michael's cemetery and see Drew's grave. We only have another forty-five minutes or so before the sun goes down and the cemetery closes. I run from the train through the pouring rain to my sister's car. The windshield wipers are on their fastest speed, and each time they wipe the pounding rain away, I can see her expressionless face staring at the concrete steps leading down the tracks into the parking lot. We haven't had a real conversation in any sense of the word since her "vacation" to San Francisco.

I get in the car. We don't say hi to each other. She just pulls away from the curb and takes me where I need to go like a taxi driver. I maneuver my feet around the skateboard and basketball on the floor of the car and settle in for the fifteen-minute drive to Saint Michael's.

As we near my destination, I finally speak. "You didn't tell Mom I was coming, did you 'Chelle?"

"No, Christian. I'm not an idiot." The exasperation in her voice is palpable.

"Just double-checking."

"Why are you coming here, anyways? You haven't visited Drew's grave more than once since he di—"

"Shut the fuck up, Michelle. If you didn't want to pick me up, you didn't have to. I really don't need the third degree."

"Fine, whatever," she says, rolling her eyes.

We pull into the cemetery. The pounding rain has reverted to a light drizzle. The drops are tiny eyeballs hitting the windshield. Their lives splatter instantly, but not before they steal a look at my face. Michelle drives straight until we reach an island in the road that features a large marble sculpture of Jesus rising from the dead. We make a full circle around it and pull over to the curb on the right. Drew's headstone is three plots in. Mom chose a flat slab level with the ground opposed to the traditional standing headstone. I open the passenger door, step out and remain motionless next to the car as if I've been super-glued to it. Michelle stays in but rolls down both front windows while I look up into the dark gray sky, as thousands of miniscule eyes die on my forehead. I hear her light a cigarette. Reaching into the car through the passenger window, I snatch it out of her hand and chuck it out the driver's side window.

"Who do you think you are?!"

"Since when do you smoke?"

"Since none of your business." She gets out of the car, walks around to the rear of it and sits on the bumper.

"Michelle, you're seventeen years old and—"

"So what? You were smoking when you were twelve."

"And I quit! Besides, you're on the girl's basketball team *and* the cheerleading team. Do you want to mess up a potentially full scholarship because you fucked up your lungs?"

She crosses her arms. "Yeah, well, it's either that or get pregnant or get fat or shoot heroin." Her eyes tear up. "Fuck you, Christian. I may be seventeen, but I'm more mature than you will be ten years from now."

I let out a sigh and try to change the subject. "How's Mom?"

"How do you think? She keeps telling me I need to go to confession and pray for my sins, not to mention yours. During dinner one night last week, I told her I wasn't going to say grace with her. We started screaming, and she was chasing me around the house."

I apply pressure with my thumb and pointer finger to the pain growing above my forehead.

"I locked myself in my room. I saw her sleeping at the kitchen table in the morning. And all her old photo albums were on the table. I made breakfast and went to school."

I see the faint lights of the utility vehicle driven by the caretaker at the other end of the cemetery. He's locking the gates on that end and will probably make his way through the yards, row by row, until he's certain everyone has left. He'll get to us in less than fifteen minutes.

"Michelle you have to get out of that house. I love Mom, but she needs help."

"You want me to run away like you did? Someone has to take care of her. I can't give up on my family as easily as you."

"You don't know what I've been through."

"All I know is you haven't been around in years. I don't even know who you are. You're supposed to be my big brother, but you're not. You don't care about me. You don't care about Mom. All you care about is a father you never knew and a boy rotting in a grave who hated you when he was alive."

I slap her across the face. Hard. She returns the sign of affection. It stings.

"If Andrew knew you were a fag, he would've jumped in front of that car."

"Fuck you!"

"Fuck you, too. Fucking faggot." She lights another cigarette.

I slap her in the face again, knocking the cigarette out of her mouth. The embers flake onto her jean-jacket and quickly burn out amid the ocular carnage that has fallen from the evening sky. She spots a loose rock in the grass and frantically charges toward it. She holds it over her head, preparing to throw it at mine. At the last second, she freezes. Her arm shakes until the rock drops from her hand and thuds to the ground. She begins sobbing and collapses, her wails echoing against the headstones. They bounce against the concrete and marble until it flees to the busy streets of industrial Bridgeport. Running to my sister, I hug her. I tell this stranger I love her, I'm sorry, I'm going to be around more. I'm going to work things out with Mom. I want to help.

We sit in the wet grass while my jeans begin to dampen. The caretaker has reached our car. He flashes his lights to signal that we have to leave the premises. The eyes turn into raindrops again. We leave the cemetery. I never do visit my dead brother.

SEVENTEEN

“ Mr. White, I'm going to have to ask you to leave. You tell me you have information about Juan Carlos' murder, and yet you've been the most uncooperative voluntary informant I have ever dealt with. See, the way this works is you talk and I listen. If you're going to sit there tight-lipped and in a daze, then I'd rather go to lunch.” He looks at me inquisitively. “You saw the reward offered, and you want to get paid, right?”

I remain silent.

He smirks. “Yeah, that's what I thought. Now get the fuck out of my office before I arrest you for wasting my time.”

Officer Flap opens the office door. I concentrate on the slicing sound the white metal blinds make as they swing gently back and forth, and I want to tell him who I am and what I've done, but something holds me back.

One of the things I fear most is becoming my father, and now that it's happened I'm having trouble making it public. I don't feel bad about murdering Juan Carlos. On the contrary, part of me wishes I remembered the gory details, as if I'd covered my eyes at a horror movie and then regretted it later. It's just that I'm terrified of the looks that will come across my family's faces when my mother discovers what I've become, when I'm not the tortured soul my sister has made me out to be. I'm a drug addict, a whore and a murderer, and soon enough everyone will know it.

A young man who looks close to my age is flailing his legs as he's dragged into the station by three officers while he belts out, “It wasn't me! It wasn't me! Goddammit, let me go! Why won't you listen to me?" He breaks down in tears as his body goes limp. I'll tell the police tomorrow.

EIGHTEEN

Since I was a kid, I've gotten myself into huge amounts of trouble and felt extremely guilty about it afterward. The trouble seems to just get worse as I grow older, as does the responsibility I burden myself with and the hatred I turn inward. I'm pretty sure I'm this way because I was raised a Catholic.

While we were parishioners and students at St. Ambrose, my brother and I were able to leave school to assist the priest when he administered funerals during the weekdays. After mass it was customary for the family to tip the priest and altar boys. We'd make anywhere from five to twenty bucks.

During the mass, we'd prepare the incense and hold the bible for the priest. We'd carry the cross while leading the initial procession of mourners down the aisle and to the altar. Typically, Drew would carry the burden of the heavy cross because I wasn't strong enough. An average of ten altar boys helped at Saint Ambrose Church, and the shifts were assigned evenly by the two parish priests, Fathers Garcia and Montana.

Father Garcia was the youngest of the pair. He was tall, with a medium build, olive skin, dark features, in his early thirties. Father Montana was in his late fifties, bald, short and overweight. Both priests were kind. Father Garcia's charismatic, easygoing approach to the parishioners complimented Father Montana's conservative ways.

I took extra care when working at a funeral over which Father Montana was presiding. The amount of our tip was based on how closely our performance adhered to his rules. He'd monitor our preparation of the bland wafers and red wine. During the mass, half of his brain would be concentrating on prayer while the other was keeping an eye on my counterpart and me to see if we were goofing off. At the end, before leaving the church, he'd double-check that we'd completed our duties such as stowing the wineglass, plate and incense, wiping the altar down, and closing the bible. He'd wait until we were finished and then walk the two of us back to school so we could return to class without causing mischief. Only on rare occasions would he thank us.

Father Garcia poked fun at the seriousness of death when overseeing a funeral. His optimistic approach to tragedy was what afforded him preference with the parishioners, but there were a large number of old-fashioned churchgoers who were stuck in the traditional ways of Father Montana.

At the end of a funeral, Father Garcia tended to race back to the convent to watch television, leaving us to our own devices. Once alone, Drew and I would ransack the closets. We'd pull out the bag of crucifix-stamped wafers and mock the priests. I'd hold the bread up in the air and repeat the words "the Body of Christ" in a strained, deep voice. We'd share a glass of the wine, although we usually wouldn't drink much because we didn't like the taste. But once when we had, we peed into the carafe so nobody would notice that the level of the wine had been lowered. Large, tarnished, silver canisters would be filled with incense that we'd burn while running down the aisles of the church, swinging them by their chains and chanting.

After twenty minutes of silliness, we'd clean up as if Father Montana were scrutinizing our every move. The short walk back to Saint Ambrose Elementary would be consumed with giggling, shoving, and our pockets would be holding dollar bills. We'd greet our teacher with the smell of cheap red wine on our breath and the intoxicating aroma of the holy incense embedded in our school uniforms.

NINETEEN

“ Hey, dude. What do you think the key to success is?”

Disinterestedly, I answer. “I don't know. An education?”

He nudges my side with a closed fist. “No cigar! Try again!”

Before I have a chance to humor Hartley with another vague response, he cuts me off.

“You gotta follow the wisdom, man. Seriously. If you want to get anywhere in life, you need one thing and one thing only.”

“What is it, Hart. Tell me.”

“A tan!”

He leans against my kitchen counter with inexcusable confidence. I stare at him, dumbfounded by his existence.

“Listen to me, man, and you'll go places,” he instructs as he whips out a business card to Hollywood Tans and shoves it in my face.

I hold back laughter. “That's an interesting hypothesis.”

He sips his vodka on the rocks. “It's not a hypothesis. It's a fact, my friend. With a decent base tan, you can beat the obstacles of people and circumstances in your life, and you'll make it anywhere.”

I offer him a teeth-clenched smile. “You should write a book or become one of those motivational speakers.”

“I'm good, right, dude?”

Hartley has come over after dinner at yet another Japanese restaurant. I'm staring at the mouse stain on the floor and think I can make out the vague imprint of his Sketcher sneaker treads in it. His clients are obvious fans of Asian cuisine. His clothes reek of food. He chews gum with the failed hopes of neutralizing his breath from the pot stickers he ate earlier. I kiss him and taste his meal.

He stops abruptly and with seriousness asks, "You're not gonna flip out over a dead rat again, are you?"

"It was a mouse, and no, I'm not. I was just having a bad week."

He makes an expression of relief, kisses me again.

We blow each other. After sex we dress and take a ride in his BMW to the ATM a block and a half away. He pays me at my usual rate. We stop at Tasti-Delite on Second Avenue where we both order kiddie-size cups of marshmallow-flavored ice cream.

"This stuff rules," he says and orders a quart for his wife and children. He drops me back home hastily and heads for Long Island in a race with the melting ice cream.

TWENTY

Billy is about six inches shorter than I am but stockier. He's kind
of cute, I think to myself as I step inside to let him into my
apartment. His preppy clothes and tousled, longish brown hair make
up for his tiny gut and slightly unshaven beard. My smile comes
and goes at a rapid rate, the way it tends to do when I'm around
strangers. The left side of my smile quivers and jumps up in pursuit
of the right side. Then it all comes down.

He speaks. "So where do you want to do it?"

As usual, I steer him toward the blowjob dish chair and I sit on
the floor between his hairy legs. Just before I'm about to go down, our
eyes connect for a split second. He looks at me as if he wants to know
something about me. Avoiding his glance, I smile uncomfortably,
open my mouth and lower my head.

Billy text messages me: "You around tonight?"

I type a slow reply, using the numbered keypad on my cell phone:
"How about you come over in thirty min?"

"See you then."

Luckily, I just finished exercising. I light a candle, take a quick
shower and shave. As I'm blow-drying my hair, I get another text:
"You into anything else besides oral?"

Curious, in text format, I ask, "Like what?"

"Like making out or fucking?"

"We can make out."

Not even five minutes later, he's buzzing my bell. When I open the door, he gives me another one of those dreamy eye stares. I return his look with a furtive glance. My eyes are fixed on the dust balls that are caught between the wiring that travels along the hardwood floors into all of the electronic equipment. He breaks my daze by slamming his semi-dry lips against my moist lips. Our saliva mixes as the butterflies in my stomach flutter a message to my brain, telling me he's a good kisser. I internally curse myself for obliging his make-out request. If I'm not getting paid to do it, I consider kissing much more intimate than fellatio or sodomy. He pushes me gently up against one of the metal legs on my loft bed, never taking his mouth off mine. As much as I appreciate his intimate gesture, I find my heart closed to anything like this, so in conflict with my primitive carnal needs.

"You wanna go up top?" He points to the loft bed.

"Okay."

He hurriedly takes off his clothes and helps me remove mine. I climb the ladder to my bed, and he chases after me. I lie down and he plops on top of me, searching sloppily for my mouth with his eyes closed. He continues to kiss me, and I feel the burning passion in the way his lips move, his breathing, his body. At this point I just want to make him cum fast so he can get dressed and get out. But I don't want to be rude. I'll wait it out.

Panting, he asks me, "Do you feel anything?"

I know he's talking about the chemical connection between us, but in an effort to demonstrate emotional disinterest, I reply with, "Feel what? Your dick?"

"No, this."

He kisses me again, and I do feel it. It's such an odd, nonsexual feeling. I don't know this man. I met him online for fuck's sake, but unfortunately the emotional attraction I feel is uncontrollable. Finally I give into the feeling and press my body into his, all the while thinking with my heart: How long will we be together? What if it doesn't work out? Does he have a girlfriend and play the straight life as well? What if he starts to think I'm not attractive anymore? And when we go out, will people think he's good-looking enough? Wait a minute, what if they think he's too hot? Will he be faithful?

I have a talent for playing out and ending a relationship in my brain before it even happens. It can be a bad thing or a good thing. Considering instances like this when I'm having an emotionally immature moment, I consider it a good thing.

In an internal panic, I give him one of my turbo-speed blowjobs to provoke a rapid orgasm. Success: It sprays all over my face, creating what's proverbially known as a "facial" in the gay community, and doesn't get in my eyes. As I'm wiping myself off with a paper towel and taking a Listerine swig over the bathroom sink, I feel hands grab either side of my torso, Billy's bare chest pressing against my perspiring back.

"That was fucking awesome, man." He kisses my neck and I stiffen.

"No problem," I say and turn to face him with one of my signature smiles. "I don't want to kick you out, but I've got a lot of stuff to do."

I smile as he edges backward out my front door. It prompts him to lunge at my face for one last kiss, but before my lips can form a smooch, he's tonguing my exposed teeth. Disgusted, I wave goodbye as he strides down the hall of my building and out the front entrance onto the city sidewalk, I'm sure doing nothing but thinking of our bright future. I will not see him again.

TWENTY-ONE

When I think of a guy named Reginald who's from Brooklyn, I create in my mind a vivid picture of an overweight black man in his forties. When I meet Reginald standing at my door, I see an average-looking Caucasian man in his late twenties with a mild beer belly and reddish brown hair. He's wearing a green and white New York Jets jersey, baggy blue Levis and black Timberland boots. He says hello and asks me to call him Reg.

He's twirling his large keychain round and round on his thick pointer finger. Watching him play with the keychain, I can almost be certain he treats his handcuffs in the same fashion, but he's not in his police uniform this sunny Sunday afternoon. He's not here on official business.

He asks me to turn off the lights. As I suck his cock, he inquires over and over again whether I like it when he squeezes the life out of my ass cheek as if he were popping a monstrous whitehead. I lie and say yes. In the past, I might've been turned on by such rough treatment, but after the experience with Juan Carlos, and then almost being raped by those overeager dates at Nick's house during that so-called orgy, it's no longer my cup of tea. He cums in my mouth and I spit it out in the toilet.

Before I'm done gargling Listerine and washing my hands, he's dressed and gone, having left the money where I knelt mere seconds ago.

TWENTY-TWO

The water ran down my forehead like thieves, carrying with it hostages of shampoo suds, and hid in my eyes, blurring my vision.

"Where is it, Christy? Tell me where it is." Hearing the deep voice was cathartic. I recognized the voice, but I couldn't place the face.

I rubbed my eyes so I could use them to find what he was looking for. My head down, the first thing I noticed were my feet, how the milk white skin was barely visible against the eggshell-colored tub. The pinks and yellows of the toenail beds gave them away. I wished I was invisible.

I felt a wet pat on my head. I raised my head and looked to my right. Drew was in the corner of the tub, facing the sea-green-tiled walls. He was naked and standing, but with a slight shoulder hunch that suggested his muscles had contracted due to stress or pain. His legs wobbled and stiffened in an effort to correct his unstable stance.

"Drew, are you all right?" I sniffled as I asked, realizing I'd been crying.

He flinched at the mention of his name but didn't answer. Two large hands were squeezing my shoulders.

I heard the voice again. "Christy-boy, Drew did it. Now it's your turn to help me find it."

Confused, I started crying again. Where's Mommy? I wanted to ask out loud, but I thought if I did, the voice would not sound nice anymore. The big, rough hands navigated me around to face it. I found it.

"Did you find it?"

I murmured, "Yes, I found it."

It looked like a Muppet puppet. Or if a sock puppet was a living organism, that was what he'd look like under his clothes. But something in the back of my mind told me that it wasn't really a puppet. It was kinda like what Drew and I had on our bodies in the same place, although not as big or strong as the voice's.

"Good," the voice exclaimed cheerily. "You found the pink puppet!"

I heard Drew whimpering in the corner when the voice mentioned "it." I remembered seeing it before, but I didn't know why it made Drew cry. Maybe he was scared of that puppet, but I wasn't. I thought it looked funny.

"The pink puppet wants you to touch it," informed the voice as an elbow nudged me. "Go ahead. Go on, Christy-boy."

I had to use both of my tiny hands to get a firm grip on the puppet. I yanked on it with all my weight because I was hoping I could swing from it like a trapeze artist.

"Ouch!" said the voice. "Don't pull so hard."

"I'm sorry." I started crying, a sore loser.

"It's okay," the voice consoled me and patted my head again. "Do you feel how I'm patting and rubbing your head?"

I nodded.

"That's how I want you to do it to the puppet."

"Like this?" I petted it like a kitten. The puppet got bigger and stiffened.

"That's it, Christy, keep rubbing."

I did as the voice desired. The breathing got heavier.

"That's my Christy-boy. I love my Christy-boy."

My hand began to ache from the jerking. "My arm hurts," I complained.

"Aw, baby boy." The voice took my hand and began massaging the palm with a thumb.

"You can stop, anyway, 'cause the pink puppet wants you to kiss it now."

"How do I kiss it?"

"Lick it."

I did as suggested. I licked the head. There was a hint of saltiness.

"That's a good boy. Lick it a lot. Lick it faster. Faster!" The voice stuck a finger behind the sac hanging underneath and rubbed in circular motions while I kissed the sock puppet. What was inside the sac? I wondered. Maybe baby puppets?

My fingers were wrinkly, pruned from the water. We had been in the shower for such a long time. I hadn't rinsed my hair and the shampoo ran into my mouth as I licked the puppet. The bitter, salty flavor was getting icky. I stopped licking and looked up at my father. He looked down on me, puzzled, then irate.

"Don't stop, Christian!" The irritation in his voice was clear as the water.

"It tastes yucky, Daddy."

He tried to force my head onto the puppet. I wriggled away. My father raised his arm and slapped me across the face with the back of his hand, the hard, gold metal of his wedding band adding to the pain. I fell backward, hitting my big brother, who tottered to his side like a bowling pin.

I helped him to his feet as my father whispered in my ear, "You're just like your faggot brother over there."

He pulled me away from Drew, who'd retreated to his corner.

"The pink puppet is angry at you. Turn around." I faced the sea-green-tiled walls. He spread my legs with two rough kicks to my ankles and bent me over.

"Daddy, please, I'm sorry for stopping!" I cried. "I'll lick it, I'll taste it!"

He shoved something deep inside of me, filling me with searing pain. Then out. Then in again.

TWENTY-THREE

" Is this going to take long, Doctor Shivo? 'Cause my shift starts at four."

Doctor Shivo eyed my mother with patience as he adjusted his eyeglasses. "It depends, Mrs. White. What seems to be the trouble with young Christian?"

I was sitting on the examining table, my feet dangling off the side through the metal guards that prevented me from falling three feet. I was a captain on his ship. The doctor and my mother were lost at sea, conversing about me as they swam helplessly. I turned around and fiddled with the weight scale. Mom was standing in her waitress uniform and apron, arms crossed, tapping her black tennis shoe against the black and white linoleum tiles while giving me the look that said, "Stop touching everything or you're gonna get it."

"He's been bleeding when he goes to the bathroom. He forgot to flush the other day, and I saw a large amount of blood mixed with his stool."

The crinkling sound of the tissue paper I sat on was thunder, and the fluorescent lighting above me was lightning. An ocean storm was on its way. I swayed back and forth, and clung to the railing as if the imaginary waves I floated on were getting rocky.

The doctor scribbled in his notebook as he asked, "Is the blood blackish or red?"

"Red, I think."

"Does your husband's family or your own have any history of colitis or Crohn's Disease?"

"I'd have to check with Andy, but no, I don't think so."

He scribbled again and then stopped to scratch an itch in his ear with his ballpoint pen, the culprit most likely being the thick growth of gray hair inside.

"Well, we can have some blood work done. A colonoscopy is also an option, but can be very invasive for a child. Does it hurt when you go to the bathroom, Christian?"

I lied and shook my head no. I didn't want my mother to know about the pink puppet. She brushed my hair back, then licked a tissue and wiped sticky residue off my cheek from a lollipop the nurse had given me to eat in the waiting room.

"Mrs. White, children are susceptible to small cuts in the anal cavity. Christian doesn't seem to be in any pain. It may be so small he doesn't feel it."

"So what do you suggest I do?"

"Give him a tablespoon of mineral oil and a glass of prune juice twice a day. This will soften his stool and prevent constipation so the wound can heal without further damage or complications." The doctor jotted down his prescription, handed it to my mother and said, "If the bleeding continues or gets worse, please bring young Christian back in for testing."

Mom folded the note and put it inside her black acrylic purse. "Thank you, Doctor."

"My pleasure. How's your eldest, Andrew?"

"Well, he's been a little weird. Christian, let's go."

I aborted ship. Doctor Shivo picked up his clipboard and opened the exit from the ocean for us.

"Has he started school?"

"No, next week."

"Soon you won't have to pay the babysitter." He chuckled.

We walked down the hall to the front desk so my mother could pay. The children playing and the babies writhing in the waiting room were beached fishes, crabs and snails.

Mom signed a check, tore it from the book and handed it to the nurse as she responded to the doctor. "He's not with a sitter. He's home with his father."

TWENTY-FOUR

My past comes to me in daydreams like nightmares I haven't had since I was younger. I used to have this one dream about my mother almost every night. She'd be kidnapped by two dark men. They resembled Peter Pan's shadow, except there were two of them. Throughout the night, I searched the dream for my mother, and just before I awoke, I'd find her assailants standing in front of McDonald's. I'd beg and plead for them to tell me where she was. They'd laugh in my face and hand me an old cigar box, informing me that its contents were all that was left of her. I'd slowly open the mini-chest and inside was a single green pea. Then I'd wake up crying. The nightmare recurred at least once or twice a week for most of my childhood.

Not that suddenly recalling my father fucking Drew and me in the bathroom when I was a toddler isn't worse than my green pea-mom nightmare. It's just that as I've been staring at the young mother with her two boys at the grocery store, I've been bombarded with nightmares, most of which are my past disguised as daydreams.

I don't want to become my father. The sordid sexual situations I've put myself in, the drugs, Juan Carlos, I suddenly feel like they're all precursors to becoming something despicable, someone I now see I was intended to become. I look at how unaffected the two sons are, how one rides in the metal shopping cart and the other pushes while their mother gives them a loving look of disapproval.

Sometimes I'm still five. I see snippets of my young self as he looks through the bars I've kept him behind all these years. My dead brother sits next to him. I can't do this forever. I can't keep selling myself and selling myself because when the time comes for it to matter I will have nothing left to give. I will truly be nothing. It's time to let my father go. It's time to let Andrew go. It's time to turn myself into the police and tell them everything I know about Juan Carlos' death.

"It's time to go," I exhale along with a few wet whimpers.

"Go where? Where are you going to go?" the younger son inquires, his long, disheveled, dirty-blond hair spilling back as he looks up at me.

I smile and start to respond, but before I do, the protective mother snatches the boy away. She throws me a friendly glance as she turns the corner at the end of the aisle while reminding her son to never talk to strangers.

PART THREE
THE FATHER

ONE

I'm being questioned in a room with a two-way mirror. Knowing there are police on the other side of it should make me uncomfortable, but I'm not. What's more, the name of the man interrogating me is Reginald Jenkins, a repeat customer of mine. I stress repeat and not regular because our visits have been brief, impersonal and infrequent.

He stomps into the room like an accusing moose, but freezes mid-step when he recognizes my face. How do I play this? We know each other, but I decide to act as if we don't for the time being.

"You're a detective?"

"Yes, I'm Detective Reginald Jenkins." Seeing me has made him sit down in slow motion, as if he's lowering an injured ass onto a red blowup ring.

"You're pretty young to be a detective."

"Let's just stick to Juan Carlos," he snipes without looking at me.

"If I stayed stuck to Juan Carlos, I'd be dead by now." My feet fumble anxiously on the floor like the hind paws of Thumper in the classic Disney cartoon, *Bambi*.

"Why don't you tell me what you just told Officer Flap? Just give it to me straight. I don't want to hear any of that spiritual crap you laid on the other detectives."

I want to be defiant. But I'm tired and want it all to be done. I tell him about how I was broke, the night out drinking alone, and meeting Juan on my way to the home I used to share with Gelly. He demands specific times, what clothes I wore, what drinks I drank. I tell him about the sex-suggestive deal we made, the glass and steel penthouse, and the antique furniture.

"And then what happened?"

"He told me to take my clothes off, and so I did."

He shifts in his chair. "Yes?"

"He had me turn around..."

He responds to my hesitation with another "yes." I can't help but suspect my story is turning him on. His hazel eyes have a hint of horny green.

"He laid me on his lap and began spanking me."

"Why?"

"He said it was because I was bad. I played along until he started punching my back. I jumped up and ran for the door, but he stopped me. I turned around, and he punched me in the face. It knocked me out."

"And is that the last thing you remember?"

I had a dream about Kurt Cobain last night. We were in a square room with beige carpeting, and there was wood paneling on the walls. He was sitting clumsily in a rocking chair, wearing his signature flannel shirt and ripped jeans. He strummed on an acoustic guitar and stared at me as I sat cross-legged in the opposite corner, transfixed by his presence. He kept singing the same line over and over from the song "Sifting" on his first album *Bleach*: "Don't have nothing for you! Don't have nothing for you! Don't have nothing for you!" Courtney Love stood in the corner with some nerd, screaming over and over, "What? You think I killed him? You asshole!"

"Christian!" He snaps his fingers. "Is that the last thing you remember?"

I see a cockroach running along the length of the wall underneath the two-way mirror.

"No."

Reg sighs. "Okay so what else you got?"

I rehash my last flashback. I tell him about waking bound to the bedposts, how Juan tied my ankles to the floor. I tell him how he fucked me with a broken beer bottle, and how the pain made me pass out again.

"It's been coming back in segments. I can't remember everything. That's the last thing."

"You don't remember murdering him?"

"I didn't fucking murder him. It was self-defense. I don't remember, but I know it was."

He tosses a folder across the table, and photographs of Juan's body slide out of it and onto my lap. "You call that self-defense?"

The 8½-by-11 color photographs depict a gruesome scene.

"This isn't the way the newspapers said it happened."

"We censored some of the details."

"This wasn't me. I couldn't have done this."

In the pictures Juan is lying facedown in bed like the paper said, but his arms have been severed and are tied to either of the bedposts. In another photo, his body has been flipped over by the police to reveal a badly beaten head and upper torso, along with a stab wound to the chest. A white bowling pin rests at his feet, looking as if it had been dipped in a basin of blood.

"You came in here today to make a confession. Now that you see your handiwork, you're going to deny being guilty? What happened, Christian, he didn't pay you or stick that bottle deep enough to get you off?"

My temper flares, "Fuck you, *Reg*. I don't remember, but if I did anything, it would be to escape. I didn't come here to confess. Shit, I came here to tell you what happened!"

"I told you my name is Reginald."

"That wasn't your name before."

His face flushes a crimson red like an angry *Looney Tunes* cartoon about to blow. He stiffens and dares me with his eyes to make another comment like that. He thumbs through his notes, searching for something, but can't find it because his mind is muddled by my accusation. Without notice, the door opens slowly until an officer pokes his head in.

"Reg, could you step outside a moment?"

Reg keeps his eyes on me while he follows the other officer's request. As he leaves, a female cop snatches the file and notes from his hand and enters. She sits back in the chair and leafs through the paperwork.

In a matter-of-fact tone she speaks. "I'm Detective Rojas. Do you have anything more to add, Mr. White?"

"I came here to tell you what happened, but…those pictures," I swallow, "I didn't do that."

The officer has bleached blond hair pulled tightly back in a ponytail. Her body is curvy, voluptuous but not fat. She purses her fire-engine red lips and then says, "But you don't remember what happened after the rape. People black out when something traumatic happens. It's most likely you lost control after he was abusing you, and you wanted to get back at him. So you tied him up like he did to you. You stuck him with a knife and beat him to death with the bowling pin he was about to rape you with. Then you cut off his arms that he was using to hurt you. "

"No, that's not true." My heart is beating the inside of my chest like the instrument that bludgeoned Juan over and over.

"There are prints all over the bowling pin that will no doubt match yours. We're still looking for the knife. It'd be helpful to you if you cooperated with us and told us where we could find it."

I stand up like lightning, pushing the chair back against the wall.

"What knife, what are you talking about?"

The impact of the chair on the wall startles the cockroach into another run. I watch him bolt through the crack under the door. Detective Rojas rises as the perpetrator escapes. I want to tell her I wish I was his size, but she probably wouldn't get it.

"Christian White," she says in a slight Puerto Rican accent as she snails her way toward my side of the room, "you are under arrest for the murder of Juan Carlos."

She turns me around and handcuffs me. I don't struggle. Two officers enter the room.

"Anything you say can and will be used against you in a court of law."

One of the cops looks like my father.
"You have the right to an attorney."
And he's coming to take me away.

TWO

My father was convicted of murder in the first degree exactly one month before my seventh birthday. Precisely one week before that, he was sentenced to twenty-five years to life in a maximum security prison in upstate Connecticut with the possibility of parole in fifteen years, and also was required to complete a drug rehabilitation program.

Mom divorced my father six months prior to his arrest for the murder of Robert Roosevelt. When they locked him up, she brought my brother and me to live with her father. The police took her in for questioning, and she cooperated completely, thereby offering vital evidence and testimony that led to his conviction.

When my father hadn't been fucking Drew and me, he was beating my mother or selling drugs. On many occasions, he'd drug her before bed so she slept through the night while he stole our household appliances to sell on the street for drugs or money. He'd act sweet as a lollipop while offering her a hot cup of tea filled with tranquilizers. She'd drink it with gratitude, naïve as she was.

Mary, my mother's best friend and pseudo-sister, saved my mother's life on a regular basis. There was one particular incident when she walked in on my father strangling my mother. He had her pinned against the wall in the living room between two potted plants smashed on either side of them, the dirt turning the white carpet a dry shit color. They'd fallen off the television when he threw her against it for asking him what he'd done with the washing machine.

Mary was a tough woman, and it took her no more than two

seconds to fling my crackhead skinny father off my mother and across the room. He bolted out the front door. She insisted Mom call the police, but she refused like always. Her pale face had a tinge of blue, and purple bruising was already forming around her neck.

Aunt Lynda, my father's sister, lived on the other side of the two-family house. She was five feet away from the back screen door, sunning herself in the hot and humid afternoon, the rays burning her blotchy skin. Mom had been screaming for help at the top of her lungs while my father tried to kill her. Aunt Lynda hated Mom. She was jealous of her beauty and the attention she took away from the brother she loved perhaps too much.

After my father went to jail, Mom would tell us he was in California. My memories of him abusing me would come and go. At times I missed him, and at other times I was scared he'd come back. Even though he was in jail and had undergone treatment for drugs, she was still fearful of him and his fucked-up family. Aunt Lynda insisted my brother and I be brought to his sentencing to say goodbye.

My father had grown a beard and gained weight. I remember telling him he looked like a young Santa Claus. He picked me up as I laughed with joy, and while Drew solemnly stood by. He never forgot what our father did to us. My father told us he was going away on vacation, and he'd be back soon. Neither of our parents told us about the murder he committed, nor did our mother tell us that our father had threatened to find her and kill her after he was released for testifying against him in court.

Drew and I called my father's mother "Nauny." He acted and dressed younger than she was. She dyed her graying hair black and wore tight-fitting clothing. She'd tan on a regular basis, and her skin was alligator-leathery. She was very promiscuous. The flashy, mafia-affiliated men with whom she associated made my father envious. Their designer suits and expensive cars caused him to feel inferior. At the time, he was only driving a truck that delivered coffee beans. His hunger for more caused him to start selling and eventually using cocaine. He quit his job in coffee and began working illegally fulltime.

His addiction changed his persona. My mother, Drew and I were constant outlets for his rage. He relieved himself on us like we were human toilets. Most things about him, including the abuse, I haven't always been able to remember, but what I can haunts me to this day.

When there were no more appliances left in our house, my father decided to ask a friend for a loan. He bought a gun off the street in downtown Bridgeport and went to Robert Roosevelt's home in Stratford. Being close friends with my parents since childhood, Robert was more than happy to invite my father in when he knocked on the front door. I've always imagined in great detail what happened that day based on the court documents that I stole from my mother's closet:

"I need to borrow some money, man," my father said in cocaine-laced stutters. "Just like five or six thousand, I'll get it back to you by the end of the week. I got this deal happening, and I'll double the loan like that!" He snapped his fingers.

"I don't think so, Andy," Robert said. "You still owe me the four-hundred I lent you to buy another washing machine to replace the last one you sold."

"Yeah, ma-man, but the new one fucking broke if you can believe it. I need a new dishwasher, too. Jean, waste of fucking wife she is, broke the goddamn thing before she moved out. I got water flooding the kitchen and leaking into the basement."

"You've never owned a dishwasher, and you just said it was for a deal you're putting together. What's this all about?" He put his hand on my father's tense shoulder. "You strung out on drugs, man? You've got to quit that shit. You've got kids to think about."

When he touched him, my father popped. He belted out a wild sound and whipped out an automatic firearm from the waist of his blue jeans.

"Don't fucking touch me!"

Robert toppled backward against the wall with surprise and terror. My father tackled him to the ground before he could escape. He struggled for a bit until my father knocked him out with two vicious blows to the head with the gun.

When he awoke, his hands were tied behind his back with the wire from his desk lamp. He was propped against the wall in his bedroom under the window next to the oak nightstand he'd built himself in his garage. My father was lying on the bed, mumbling to himself incoherently.

Robert jiggled his hands to test the tightness of the bind. The sound of the wire scraping against the wall snapped my father out of his meditation. He jumped up, smiling.

"Robby, Robby-boy."

"Andy, you untie me right now. You're going to get yourself into trouble."

My father's face turned bright red. "Don't tell me what to fucking do! I make the rules. I'm in charge here!"

He yanked the gun from his waist and pulled Robert's head back with his left hand by sticking his pointer and middle fingers into Robert's nostrils. He jammed the gun into Robert's mouth with such immense force that he shattered his two front teeth.

"You like sucking on that? I bet you do, you fucking faggot. Now, are you going to be quiet?"

He nodded, and when he did, the blood from his mouth streamed down his face faster, and dripped onto the blue carpet, staining it a deep purple. My father ripped the pistol from his victim's mouth and blood poured out as if from a faucet.

"All you had to do was give me the money. I didn't come here for another one of your hypocritical interventions. I'm sick of people telling me what to do. I'm the man, and I'm going to start getting treated as one, or I'm going to have to start proving it."

"You're the man, Andy," gurgled Robert.

My father laughed at the pathetic way Robert looked and sounded. "That's right. I'm the man. I'm God." He pointed the gun at him.

Robert pleaded for his life. "I'm sorry, Andy! We can go to the bank right now, however much you need. It's all yours. You don't have to do this."

My father tapped his own forehead with the tip of the gun and chuckled.

"I can't lie. Sure, I came for your money, but what I really want is respect."

"I respect you!"

"If I keep letting lowlifes like you give me the runaround, I'll go back to driving that coffee truck for the rest of my life."

"There are other ways! It doesn't have to be like this!"

My father didn't blink. In cold blood, he pulled the trigger, releasing a single bullet into the forehead of Robert Roosevelt.

THREE

I hang up on my mother before she has a chance to berate me for the third time this week. Over the jail's phone, we've been arguing back and forth about the lawyer, the money, the murder. I don't know how to explain to her my reasons for killing this man. My inability to remember the specifics of how I did it torments her even more than what she thinks of as my multiple acts against God. The media is swarming around the case because of Juan Carlos' family fame. My mother's lawyer, Gerard Jones, who has already cost her a couple thousand, is hesitant about moving forward because of my amnesia about the gruesome details of the murder. He's been dedicated to my mother's legal woes since her divorce from my biological father, so it's extremely disconcerting that he has doubts about helping me.

Michelle is pregnant. My mother told me how my sister changed after my last visit practically overnight. I guess my sister told her about our argument at the cemetery. Michelle misconstrued my reconciliation with the promise to move home. When I didn't come, she started acting out by fucking half the members of a local gang. Now she's two months pregnant and has no clue who the father is. The scholarships and acceptance letters to Ivy League colleges such as Yale and Princeton keep piling up in the mailbox, but my sister is focused on having a baby. I know she's doing this to get back at me. If I could just talk to her, sit her down and tell her that she'll ruin her life if she has that baby. Mom asks Michelle to call me, but she refuses. I have to get out of here.

As my hand lifts from the black receiver, Gal, the Israeli jail guard, takes hold of my wrist and escorts me down the hall to my single cell in the Bernard B. Kerik Complex. I count the number of tiles on the floor on the way to my cell and come up with twenty two. As Gal locks the cell door, I wipe the tears from my eyes with the sleeve of my oversized, bright orange jumpsuit.

The Kerik Complex has been renovated recently. I inhale the fresh, storm-colored paint. The fumes kill the brain cells I need to figure out why I decided to turn myself in when the police had no clues or evidence that would have implicated me in the murder. Now, of course, they have my fingerprints to use as a match. Secondly, I'm certain I'm not the first man to be tortured and raped by Juan. He could still be out there hurting vulnerable people had I not done the world a favor. I felt that by turning myself into the authorities and making a statement of what I was able to remember, the police would have no choice but to agree it was self-defense, but the nature of the counterattack on Juan created skepticism about the validity of my claims.

Mom has offered to post bail if I spend the time in between court dates at home. I've refused. My next hearing isn't for two weeks. I'll be spending the hours thinking about what I cannot remember. Tomorrow, Gerard is supposed to visit. I have to sign some preliminary paperwork and begin building my defense because he's almost certain this will go to trial. At the arraignment, I pled not guilty to the charge of voluntary manslaughter and no contest to the charge of prostitution.

Voluntary manslaughter is defined as an intentional killing that the offender had no prior intention of doing. The circumstances leading to the homicide must be the kind that would cause a levelheaded person to become emotionally or mentally disturbed.

The memory of that night has come back in snippets, the last I remember involving Juan sodomizing me with a chipped beer bottle.

It was self-defense no matter how you cut it.

FOUR

The cab driver, Monty Nunez, picked up my father on the corner of Noble Avenue and Old Town Road at around 10 p.m. How my father spent the four hours between the time of the murder and the time he left the scene of the crime is still unknown.

A plump Mexican in his fifties, Monty was wearing a powder-blue, buttoned-down shirt and khaki pants.

The first thing Monty noticed about his customer was that his face and clothes were splattered with tiny droplets of red he assumed to be paint. The customer's eyes were puffy, and darkness circled the edges.

"Where to?"

My father, distant, stared out the window. "New York City."

"Right away. That's a pretty hefty fare. I could keep the meter running or charge you a flat rate of a hundred bucks."

In monotone, my father replied, "That's fine. I have plenty of money."

Most of the ride to the city was quiet. Monty glared at the passenger in the rearview mirror. My father was sleeping and beginning to snore. His coked-out nose began bleeding and dripped on the freshly cleaned vinyl seats.

"Hey, buddy, wake up! You're bleeding all over my goddamn car seat!"

My father sat up and wiped his nose with the white T-shirt he was wearing.

"Oh, I'm sorry man, allergies, you know."

Monty handed him a tissue. "Just wipe it up good. I don't want a mess in my cab. I just had it cleaned."

"Sorry, man," apologized my father as he obediently cleaned his mess.

"Is that how you got all those stains on your shirt and face?"

My father gazed at his reflection in the glare of the window and saw the blood of his victim, which looked as if it had been sprayed on him. He laughed.

"What's so funny?"

After a good thirty seconds of cackling, my father confessed to Monty while driving to New York on I-95 South.

"I killed a man today."

"Yeah, you're just yanking my chain. What is it, paint?" he asked as he continued down the highway at a reasonable speed of sixty miles per hour.

"It's blood, man," said my father as he solidified his avowal with an icy eye connection through the rearview mirror.

Monty saw the look in my father's eyes and knew he was telling the truth.

"No shit. You are telling the truth, aren't you?"

"That's right." My father revealed his weapon and mock shot an imaginary Robert Roosevelt. "Bang! And that was it. Pieces of his brain and blood were all over the place. The little fucking pussy popped like a pumpkin, man. He claimed we was going to go to the cash machine, but I trashed his house and found a big stash of it and left."

The sight of the gun caused Monty's heartbeat to elevate. "So why'd you do it?"

My father looked out the window again as he spoke. "People just don't understand anymore, you know? I mean take you. You're a perfect example. You work for measly amounts of money while lowlifes with luck feel they can walk all over you. That's why I did it, man. It's time to show the world what I'm made of.

"I've hooked that loser-fuck up with coke so many times. Just 'cause he works in Manhattan at a bank, he thinks he's some hotshot. When I ask him to borrow a couple bucks, he has the nerve to disrespect me and tell me no. After all the times I've been there for him. Doesn't he know who I am? Doesn't he know who I know?"

My father lit a cigarette and blew the smoke over Monty's Thank

You for Not Smoking sign. "He sure as fuck knows now, I'll tell ya that much."

"That's quite a story."

My father puffed on the Marlboro. "It's not a story. It's the truth. If you want respect in this world, you have to take it because no one is going to hand it to you unless you were born into it, and even then there are no guarantees."

Monty switched into the slow lane to accommodate a rude driver flashing him from behind. My father noticed substantial foliage past the emergency lane on the right side of the highway.

"Hey, man, why don't you pull over here so I can ditch this piece? I may as well get rid of it before I get to the city."

Monty pulled the bluish gray taxi into the emergency lane in the Bronx, a handful of exits away from the West Side highway in Manhattan. Vehicles whizzed by like Nascar racers. He contemplated speeding off with the other contestants while my father roamed the edge of the highway in search of the perfect place to discard his murder weapon. He decided against abandoning my father because he wanted to inform the police exactly where he dropped him off.

My father found a sewer opening close to the contaminated forest of scrawny trees and garbage that littered the embankment alongside the highway. He didn't think to wipe off his prints as he dropped the firearm into the rancid-smelling storm drain. He didn't stop to consider the eyewitness who chauffeured him to his destination.

Ten days later, he ran out of money and went back to Connecticut. He was arrested at his home based predominantly on the information provided by Monty Nunez, which included the location of the missing murder weapon and the details of what had happened.

What was most disconcerting about the tragedy is that after plentiful rest and drug recovery, my father was still unapologetic for his crime. After he was convicted of murder, before sentencing, Judge Holcomb labeled my father a "sociopath who expressed no remorse for his actions." As a result, he was punished to the fullest extent of the law.

FIVE

The seconds are centuries, the minutes millennia. The persistence of time is a nagging child, a hungry vagrant, an addict begging for more. An eye blink is an eternity. Each breath is endless. Each day is every night. Every night is every day.

The lines on the walls where the new paint cracked are barren orange trees and ladders to nowhere. I pray to a god I don't believe in for a rat or a cockroach, anyone to keep me company. Instead I talk to the dust-bunnies like Vera Donovan in Stephen King's *Dolores Claiborne*. I play with them like Baby Cow would. If only I hadn't had to give him back to the ASPCA in San Francisco when I moved back east! Maybe Gal, the nice guard, would let me keep him in my cell. We'd talk all day, and at night I'd sneak him out the window so he could find me dead leaves, just like the old days. But then he probably isn't alive anymore, the way I treated him.

I shared up until last week a cell with a fifty-year-old white man named Ralph when he attacked me for refusing to blow him. If he had money, I might've considered it. The guards had me moved to a single cell. I'd rather be with the other prisoners.

When I broke up with Cale and was crying everyday, Nina, the girlfriend of Nathan, the dealer who lived in Potrero Hill, gave me some words of comfort one day while we were driving in her Range Rover to a poetry slam at the Justice League.

She said, "There's something beautiful in the purity of pain."

I'd rather bleed than lie here another moment. I'd rather cry than do nothing, feel nothing, be nothing. I think of my father. I wonder if he's doing the same thing right now, lying in his cell in Osborn, feeling sorry for himself. Maybe he's writing me another letter while the dozens he's already sent are being forwarded back to him.

And then I think of being fourteen again, and of the funeral. At it my mother was trying to hold me up but the effort had reversed without her noticing. She was over a foot taller than me, but she hung on my side, a grieving ornament dressed in black. She dangled from my shoulder as I led the procession to the altar. My big brother followed perpendicular, encased in wood.

The Saint Ambrose youth choir on the balcony behind us hummed a hymn as hundreds of friends and relatives filled the church. Dozens upon dozens of mourners stood outside, cold and silent.

I sat my mother down. She slumped against the pew's backboard. Both Father Garcia and Father Montana presided over the service.

In unison they began. "Let us pray."

The mass proceeded like any other funeral except when it came time for me to read the eulogy. I disappointed myself when I tripped over the large marble steps that led to the altar. How could I have? I'd marched behind Drew serving funeral after funeral, and I'd never ever had a problem until now. Sensitive onlookers gasped, but I picked myself up and continued the short walk to the podium with confidence. Grief superseded embarrassment. My mother had struggled up to help me, but my stepfather, Michael, guided her back to her seat.

Staring down at the podium and the intricate design of Jesus rising from the dead etched into the wood, I took a deep breath and looked out into the audience, an inhalation heard by hundreds through the sensitive mike. Out of my pocket I pulled the folded paper with the typed eulogy, laid it out over Jesus. Then I ignored it, wiped my eyes with the sleeve of my ill-fitted suit (it was one of Drew's suits—too big).

"I'm standing here, whining that Drew is dead," I said, "and not even saying whose fault it is…"

My mother was startled out of the lethargy of her grief. She let out a piercing shriek. "Christian, it's not my fault!" She barreled toward me. To shut her out, I lowered my head, and my eyes connected with my big brother's coffin. A rush of panicky guilt flooded my lungs and stomach as my eyes tilted back into my head like Christ in His Agony.

I awoke to my mother shaking me.

"Christian! Christian! It wasn't my fault."

"I didn't mean you, Mom," I replied slowly as she helped me back to our seat. I felt eyes of sympathy on me from the crowd, and though I felt I didn't deserve it, it was calming.

After the Fathers' sermon, four male friends of my brother, one Dominican (son of Mrs. Cardoza), two Puerto Ricans and one Caucasian sang "It's So Hard to Say Goodbye to Yesterday" by Boyz II Men.

SIX

In fourth grade, my teacher taught a creative writing course for which we were required to complete and illustrate one short story per week. I was obsessed with Madonna, especially with her performance in the film *Who's That Girl*. I wrote a book called *Who's That Boy* in which the main character looked strikingly similar to me, dated Madonna and owned a pet tiger.

The first scene in the movie is her preparing for her release from prison by getting back her clothes and makeup, punching out the lesbian security guard, and hitching a ride with a stranger driving a Rolls Royce.

This all comes to mind as they hand me the two large manila envelopes that have housed the personals I was wearing and carrying at the time of my arrest. I take off the orange jumpsuit and slip on my still-crisp pair of faded, dark blue jeans. I pull my black Helmut Lang Henley over my head and shiver as the luxurious cotton caresses my torso. There are deodorant stains creating white tire marks around the armpits, but I don't mind. The black socks I wore are nowhere to be found, so I leave on the State's standard whites and cover them with my vintage pair of black motorcycle boots. The cheap black canvas and leather belt completes my old friend of an outfit. I never wear jewelry so I am officially dressed. I remove my black nylon backpack that holds my wallet and notebooks from the second manila envelope and sling it over my shoulder. I don't have a jacket with me because it was sixty–five degrees in the middle of October when I went in, but now it's almost Thanksgiving, and the temperature has dropped considerably, which is why I'm hesitant to leave Kerik before my family arrives.

My savior came in the form of Stacy Kim, a twenty-year-old Korean-American male from Albany, New York. In spite of his feminine name and pretty-boyish features, he exuded a masculine and somewhat angry demeanor. It'd be more than a month before I'd learn about him, the details of his life and the way it had interlaced with mine. Through massive coverage in local and national newspapers, on TV (including a one-on-one interview) and the Internet, I've come to know him well.

He was a medical student at New York University School of Medicine. His immigrant mother was hard on him, especially after his father died of a heart attack. She pushed him to the extreme to acquire her idea of the American Dream: medicine, law, or finance the only career paths she deemed acceptable.

He began modeling for a short period during the school term to make extra money. He did print work for both *GQ* and *Details*. It's difficult to decipher his ethnicity and impossible to conclude he's Asian, let alone Korean, without asking him. His black hair is iridescent, his white skin tinged with the pinkish hues of Korea's national flower, the *Dansim*. He reigns six-foot-three, a toned, statuesque body, fit as a Greek sculpture. His eyes are luminous gold, like a pond struck by afternoon sunlight.

He was passing his classes with straight A's up until his mother discovered he was gay. She wanted to surprise him at his East Village home for his nineteenth birthday. She paid the rent for his one-bedroom apartment (not to mention tuition) with her dead husband's life insurance policy, which is why she had her own key.

With her, she brought Stacy's favorite Korean dish, *chapchae*, which is basically sweet potato noodles with beef and vegetables. She also made a *saeng* cream birthday cake, too sweet, but very refreshing.

When she opened the front door to the apartment, she saw that all the lights were off in the kitchen and living room. Her first thought was that no one was home. Upon further inspection, she noticed a thin strip of light coming from underneath Stacy's bedroom door. She assumed he was doing his schoolwork; after all, it was a weeknight. She quietly pulled out a book of matches, inserted a single candle into the cake, and lit it. Holding the *chapchae* in one hand and the cake in the other, she used her shoulder to push the door open, and with a toothy smile, she shouted "Surprise!" in her thick Asian accent. Instead of being greeted by a grateful son, Mrs. Kim was thanked by a front-seat view of her son doggy-style-fucking a white man twice his age. The *chapchae* and lit cake dropped to the hardwood floor. Their ceramic holders shattered while pieces of fruit and beef splattered a mural of shame on the bedroom door.

Stacy had begun prostituting himself while still in medical school. Shocked by the scene, she shouted curses in Korean at her son and left.

He was too ashamed to call her. She stopped paying the rent and college tuition immediately. Within three months of the incident, he became very depressed. He dropped out of school and began selling himself fulltime.

Before he quit medical school, he'd begun stealing OxyContin and other opiates. When he ran out of the highly addictive drugs, he spent the money he earned turning tricks to buy more off the street instead of paying rent. He was quickly evicted from his home. In a matter of six months, he went from being an NYU medical student to an NYC homeless whore and addict.

Mrs. Kim had disowned him completely. She considered her son as dead as her late husband, and she mourned him.

Stacy was out of it most of the time. He spent his days in a lethargic daydream as he wandered the city. At night, he'd frequent the hotspots at the West Side piers where he could pick up married men from Jersey. The guys with the expensive cars were always an obvious best bet, but Stacy lowered his standards on dry nights to Honda and Toyota drivers. The men who made a decent salary would take him to nice hotels. They'd have dinner in expensive restaurants (after Stacy showered in the hotel room, of course) and room service for breakfast. His cheaper tricks took him to the hourly motels located on the corners of the teen streets and the West Side highway, where he blew them for fifty bucks.

There were nights when business was completely dead. Those were the nights he roamed the Lower East Side searching for "tricks on foot" as he liked to call them. One of these paying pedestrians happened to be a flashy, Caucasian senior-citizen.

He propositioned Stacy on a Lower East Side corner, the details of the interaction not unlike mine; however, it was easier to prep Stacy for torture because of his drug addiction. Juan Carlos maintained a small pharmacy in his home. He had stocks of all types of illegal substances and a large inventory of assorted pharmaceuticals, including OxyContin.

When Stacy awoke from a drug-induced slumber, his arms were tied to the bed and his feet to the floor-posts like mine had been; but instead of using the chipped beer bottle, Juan tried out a pair of pliers and the bowling pin. Stacy, in an adrenaline-infused rage, tore one of the posts out of the floor with his left foot and kicked Juan across the room.

"I'll kill you!" he screamed as the whites of his golden eyes filled with bloodshot-fury.

"I'll fucking kill you if I ever get out of here, you psycho!"

"This is for your own good, boy. You'll thank me later." Juan smiled as he filled a syringe with a clear fluid. He started toward Stacy again. "I'm paying you for your time. What I do with it is my business. It's been fun, but unfortunately, it's now time for you to go."

"Get away from me with that thing! Help! Someone help!"

With Juan on his right side, Stacy couldn't fight him off with his only free leg, the left one. Juan easily succeeded in plunging the needle into Stacy's arm.

He lulled him into an unwanted sleep: "Sshh...nobody can hear you."

Stacy awoke the following morning next to a convenience store in the Lower East Side, propped against a rusty metal cage that protected three garbage cans from the homeless and hungry. It was difficult for him to get up and walk because of the piercing pain in his rectum, but he managed to get inside the store and ask the cashier to call him an ambulance. He was admitted to New York Downtown Hospital. The nurse asked him if he'd like to report the rape to the police, but he refused, citing the injuries as due to experimental sex that went wrong. Besides, what would he tell the police anyway, that a john picked him up off the street, fed him drugs, sodomized him with a bowling pin and pulled at his insides with a pair of pliers? Why would they care?

He suffered severe anal hemorrhaging. The next morning, hours after his initial admittance, the doctors suggested he remain at the hospital to monitor the bleeding. They even prescribed him methadone to alleviate his withdrawal from OxyContin. The drugs weren't potent enough to get him high, just to hold him over. His OxyContin addiction and plans for Juan Carlos caused him to cut short his hospital visit.

He remembered exactly where Juan Carlos lived. A fire escape hung from the side of the building, but the ladder to it was almost fifteen feet from the ground. In the lobby, he climbed a water pipe to a window near the ceiling that looked out onto the fire escape. Straining to extend one leg, he smashed the glass with the heel of his leather boot. When he reached the roof, he found himself in Juan's garden. The door leading into the house was open. He crept around the room, looking for weapons and places to hide, and took a carving knife from the antique kitchen. He was in the bedroom when he heard the voices and the front door opening. He hid in the wardrobe, squeezing behind hanging white suits.

He had second thoughts about his revenge plan when he heard a second, younger voice in the bedroom. Then the violence began, and he got frightened. Tears ran down his face, and his pants became wet; he was unsure whether the dampness was being caused by blood or piss. He was paralyzed by the fresh memories of being tortured himself. He thought of his mother and imagined her cradling him in her arms like she used to when he was a boy, as she moved gently back and forth in her rocking chair, a Kim family heirloom that had been passed down by his father's mother. The last bit of his innocence left him that night.

He was jolted out of his memories by my screams of pain while Juan sodomized me with the chipped beer bottle. As I passed out and Juan came, Stacy emerged from the wardrobe. Still enjoying his intense orgasm, Juan was caught off-guard by Stacy's attack. When he turned to face him, two swift, powerful punches knocked him out. Stacy hit him in the head three more times to make sure he was unconscious. He then untied me and shook me awake. Because I was dazed, it was difficult for Stacy to understand what I was saying when he asked me for my address, but after I repeated it three times, he was able to make it out. He tied Juan's wrists to the bed frame and his ankles to the posts in the floor. Picking me up and putting my arm around his shoulder, he escorted me downstairs to the street where he hailed me a cab and told the driver my address and that I was okay, that I just had an accident and was on medication so not to worry about my injuries and sluggish state. He helped me into the cab, paid the driver, and split what was left of the three hundred dollars he had swiped from Juan's dresser drawer between him and me. "You earned this," he whispered in my ear as he slipped the remaining portion in the back pocket of my jeans before closing the cab door and sending me off.

When he got back upstairs, Juan was conscious and struggling against his bonds. He pleaded for forgiveness the entire time Stacy stabbed him in the chest, beat him to death with the bowling pin and severed both his arms.

Right after the murder, he hitchhiked home to Albany. When Mrs. Kim saw him standing at her front door, she broke down and cried, led him into the kitchen, and made him something to eat. He quit OxyContin cold-turkey and went through a horrible two-week period of withdrawal, his mother nursing him the entire time. Neither of them once brought up his homosexuality.

For the next six months, Stacy pretended that his New York City life of vice had never happened. He enrolled in an Albany community college, taking general courses while doing temporary work as an office assistant at various businesses. It was on his way to work one morning while reading the *New York Post* that he first learned about my arrest for the murder of Juan Carlos.

For the next couple of weeks, he went into a relapse, drinking every night, skipping work and classes. Mrs. Kim didn't know what to do. She confronted him late one night when he'd come home drunk yet again. She wanted to know what had caused him to suddenly change back into his old ways. They had a screaming match in Korean for less than five minutes before he broke down and told his mother everything there was to know about his addiction, prostitution and, most importantly, the murder.

Mrs. Kim felt compassion for her troubled son, whose remorse for his offenses made her want to do nothing but help him. She contacted a criminal defense lawyer named James Smith, as American a white man as she could find. Two days after Stacy turned himself in, the charges against me were dropped.

SEVEN

G al, the kind prison guard, is able to arrange for me to wait for my family in the visitor center of the complex. I thank him repeatedly as he shows me into the small, tasteless room that is empty except for a few folding chairs, a dusty plant and a wall-mounted TV that's tuned to FOX, playing old reruns of *Married with Children*. I stare fixedly at the smudgy screen, but don't pay any attention to the content of the comedy. I'm in a daze, thinking of my own family, wondering what to say to my crazy mother and pregnant sister.

"You going home?" Gal peeks his head into the fluorescent cave in which I wait.

"What do you mean?"

"I mean with your mother and sister to Connecticut?"

"That's not my home." I look away from him and try to concentrate on Christina Applegate.

"Well, look, man, uh, I was wondering, since you're being released and all, if you wanted to catch a movie sometime or something."

The actress who played Peg on the sitcom is a lesbian in real life, I think, and she's a big woman. I can only imagine her fucking submissives with a strap-on; even if she has a husband, he should be her bitch.

"Why?" I turn to watch him fidget for an answer. I never noticed how he looks until now. He's about an inch shorter than me, with buzz-cut, black hair, dark, harrowing eyes, tanned skin and an athletic body, the muscles of which seem about to rip through his uniform. He looks over his shoulder before speaking to be sure there's no one within earshot.

"I think you're cute and sweet, plus you look like you need a night out." He smiles at me like a kid at a cookie.

"Is that what you think I need, a night out? I don't know what I need, and you're gonna tell me?"

"I didn't mean to offend you, man."

"Are you even gay, Gal?"

"Yeah, but uh, not at work so let's just keep that between you and me."

"Well, I won't be around to tell the tale. Don't worry."

He clears his throat. "Should I take that as a no?"

I eyeball his hands, compare their size and shape to my own two and notice the similarities, the difference being that his are abnormally smooth for such an overtly rugged, masculine man and don't look ugly or dwarfish from any angle. I see no semblance of my father in his fingers or palms as he rubs them together in anticipation of rejection.

"When?"

"When what?"

"When did you want to go out?"

The first of the three I see is my lawyer, Gerard. He's hovering his 250-pound body over the front desk in the visitor's entrance. The glare of the cold winter sun reflects off the glass and steel doors, so when I finally see my mother following arm in arm with Michelle, it's as if they appeared in the burst of a camera flash. I search for the meaning behind my mother's mournful face. You'd think she was attending the funeral for her second son.

Her sad helplessness triggers an unexpected rage in me. What type of bad day could she possibly be having that might even come close to the hell I've been through this past year?

As the credits come up on the TV to mark the ending of a second dose of *Married with Children*, my mother is being led into the room by Gerard. She walks with the help of my sister, like a gimp. She looks up at me, and all I can think of is when she's going to start crying, but instead she grins.

"Hi, Christian."

"Mom."

"I always knew you were innocent."

"Did you? Hi, 'Chelle."

"Hi." She gives me a quizzical look, as if we're meeting for the first time.

"You look different," I tell her. Her eyes glaze over.

Gerard shakes my hand with a sturdy grip. "Happy to see you're going to be okay, son."

"Thanks." I force a smile, hating that he's called me "son."

"Are you hungry?" Mom babies. "Or do you want us all to go to your apartment, so I can cook something?"

"No, thanks. Why are you being so cheery? When I saw you walking up, you looked like somebody died."

Her happy facial features morph in milliseconds. "I just didn't want to ruin your special day."

"What are you talking about?" I examine her. Her clothes are more stylish than usual; I believe she's wearing a Kate Spade jacket. Her hair is blown out, and her makeup is less muted. I stare at her neck. "Where is it?"

"Where's what?"

"Where's that crucifix necklace you've worn since Drew died?"

She takes a deep breath. "Well, I've decided it's time for a change. I think I've been spending a little too much time with Jesus."

"Yeah, I guess you have."

"Do you like my manicure? God, I haven't had a manicure in years."

"You look great, but did I just hear you right? Did you just use the Lord's name in vain?"

Her face perks up. "Yes, I believe I did!" She reaches for me and hugs me passionately. "Christian, I want you to know that I accept you for who you are. When I thought I was going to lose you, too, I panicked. I knew in my heart that you couldn't have mutilated that man, and I feel responsible for you even having been there."

"Mom, it's not your fault. I know the difference between right and wrong."

"Yes, but what you don't know is that you have a family who loves you for you."

Michelle kisses me on the cheek. Confusion and embarrassment wash over my reddened face. Gerard stands back to give us our moment.

"This is surreal. I really don't know how to take this. So tell me, what is it that you didn't want to say because it would ruin my supposed special day?"

Mom looks at Michelle. "Should you tell him or should I?"

Courageously, Michelle spills the beans. "Okay, fine, I'm just gonna say it. Onyx died."

"How?"

"She had a severe allergic reaction to a new type of litter we were trying, had an asthma attack, and her lungs collapsed. We found her in the litter box with shit leaking out of her butt. It was all over her fur. It smelled disgusting."

Mom raises her hands in protest and says, "Alright, alright, Michelle, we get the picture. Christian hasn't even eaten yet." She dabs at her misty eyes.

"It's fine, Mom, really. Aw, that sucks though. I loved that cat."

My mother nods. "She was such a sweetie."

"She was," I agree. I wondered what all the strong emotion was about. Now I know: a cat.

Gerard grows impatient. "Okay, you three ready to get out of here and get something to eat?" He pats his rotund belly.

We all nod, a happy family. As we begin our walk out, something hits me. "Wait!"

Everyone freezes. I turn to Michelle and hold her at arm's length by her shoulders.

"What about the baby, 'Chelle?"

Through a smug smile, she answers, "What baby?"

The acid begins to rise in my stomach. "What baby? What the fuck do you mean, 'what baby'? I thought you were pregnant."

Mom digs in her purse for a cigarette and discovers a soft, crumpled pack. She stares at it for a few seconds and then tosses it and a lighter into the trash. "Ohhh, just tell him the truth, Michelle, before you give him a heart attack."

Beaming, she grasps my outstretched arms. "I had an abortion yesterday, and... I'm going to Harvard!" she shrieks with delight.

"I'm so proud of you! Congratulations!" I pull her close to me and savor the embrace.

The three of us exit Kerik's front doors and enter the bright, brisk day, my mother god-free, my sister baby-free, and me...well...free.

Detached, Gerard follows, picking his nose. I see Gal's ghostly reflection through the car windows as we walk the length of the parking lot, his eyes longing for me like Cale's once did.

EIGHT

I want you to try to imagine me as a young, happy, healthy homosexual man who enjoys his simple life of monotonous work, amateur art and an uncomplicated romance with an Israeli security guard who works at a maximum security prison. I want you to tell me that my life is good because I have a roof over my head, food in my fridge and designer clothes on my back. I want you to make me aware of the fact that I have family and friends who love me, coworkers who appreciate me, and strangers who seem to want to know me. This is all supposed to be okay. This is all supposed to be what I need. This is supposed to be life.

Who am I to want more when there are tsunamis, hurricanes and war? Who am I to feel something missing when there are those who are homeless, hungry and diseased? What is more? What is the difference between want and need? Which is wrong, if either? Which is good, if either?

I want to know what all the possibilities are for life's fulfillments so I can make an educated decision as to what type of sustenance I require. I want to read newspapers, magazines and books, watch TV and movies, wear the nicest clothes and shoes, go to school, eat at fancy restaurants and fatty fast-food chains, blow the hottest men and figure out which ones are worth it. I want to know what the fuck is going on!

I want to know why I'm racing my dead brother through Beardsley Park in Bridgeport, Connecticut. He's charging through the green landscape, up and over the hills, dodging trees and garbage cans. I'm trying to stay on the paved path while keeping one eye on him and one eye on the road. The sun is spitting golden ribbons through the park, and I avoid them so my eyes aren't blinded.

"Drew, wait up!" I call out to him, but when the words come out, they don't sound like anything at all. I'm a mute follower.

I hear him laughing the way he used to when he won any kind of competition against me. I run toward the park's exit and hop over a gigantic painted turtle as it crosses the road. Drew has already gained greater distance. I see him as a speck of rice in the grocery store's potholed parking lot.

"Wait! Don't leave me alone, please!"

My sudden fear of abandonment gains me the momentum I need to run faster. He nears the edge of the lot, stops and turns around. I freeze, too. The grain of rice enlarges as I get nearer.

"Drew, I'm coming with you!"

I see a hand waving at me. I'm not close enough to fully make out his facial expression, but I know he's smiling. He turns away again and heads for Huntington Turnpike.

"No! Drew, don't go that way! It's not safe!"

Before I can reach him, my brother has made a right onto the busy road and disappeared. Moments later, as I reach the turnpike, a red Camaro speeds past me, coming from the same place where my brother disappeared. Joker, Batman's villain, is in the driver's seat. He whizzes by, his head turned toward me with its permanent grin, paying no attention to the road. He's gone as quickly as he came.

I run right onto Huntington Turnpike in pursuit of Drew to see if he's okay. When I reach the top of the small hill, all I find is more road, bathed in an unearthly green. My road, beckoning me forward.

NINE

My mother hasn't been to church in almost six months. She doesn't need to, now that she has her Zoloft prescription. She sports fashionable clothes and a generally optimistic smile. Trying to get off the meds didn't work; she sank back into a black depression. But as long as she pops them, she's A-Okay.

Michelle is on the dean's list at Harvard. She's dating a fellow student named Isaac, a rich Jewish model slash English major who loves wearing her Victoria's Secret bras when they have sex.

For the murder, Stacy Kim was sentenced to twenty-five years in prison. I've been thinking about visiting him. Though what he did was extreme, the fact that we both suffered at the hands of Juan Carlos makes me feel connected to him, almost in a brotherly way.

Sean is being released in six weeks. He'll have three years of probation to finish, beginning at his mother's home, the luxurious house and acres that he dreads. His overbearing mother spoils any pleasure he could draw from the wealth he grew up around. He spent his hours in prison studying how to be a gold-digger because he plans on moving to L.A. (pending probation relocation approval) to "work" unassuming, old, rich fags who like to buy pretty boys pretty things.

Topher was finally sentenced: twenty-four months. He reports to a minimum security prison in Atwater, California, in two weeks. He's relieved to be going away because he's been waiting to do his time for almost two years at his parents' home in Colorado. He's not scared of prison; in fact, he's been looking forward to getting it over with. His fear stems from thoughts of his unknown future after his sentence, when he has to start a life, which can be very difficult for someone who doesn't exist.

Sean doesn't exist, either. He's just wasting time until life figures that out. Not that any of us are upset about it. There are benefits to non-existence. It's not as dramatic as it sounds. We're doing okay, and we'll be okay, even if it means nothing.

TEN

Michelle opens the car door. We don't say much, not because anything is wrong, but because there isn't anything new to talk about. Besides, we speak on the phone two or three times a week. We take Route 25 until the freeway ends and becomes road, and then we drive some more, all the way down, past the ranches and the farms, the single-room churches, and the factories, until we reach Osborn.

Describing a prison is like describing a funeral parlor. While the aesthetics may be different in different locations, the atmosphere remains the same. You can paint a hearse into a concept company car, but you'll always know that it was once used to carry the dead. You can plant flowers in front of the bland bricks, and you can hang cheap, abstract art on the yellowing white walls in the lobby, but it's still a prison, a maximum security prison to be exact, with murderers, rapists and other violent offenders.

I have her pull over and let me out before we pass the wire fence. I don't want her subjected to any more of this than she has to be. This is my thing. This is my baggage drop-off.

I register at the visitor center, sign the papers that the guard hands me, submit to a physical examination, and answer yes or no to the guard's questions. I then follow him into the visiting room. If I were able to visit Sean when he was doing time, it wouldn't have been like this. I'd have brought a roll of quarters. We would've hugged, played board games, and ate sandwiches out of the snack machine with my change while we talked shit and laughed under the hot Las Vegas sun, shading our fair skin under palm trees.

My father's skin is fair, but in a yellowy, hepatitis sort of way. He's balder than he was in the photo he sent me in San Francisco. His eyes are dark like mine. I sit in the black plastic chair but he remains standing, taking me in, examining me. I keep my fidgety hands below the table, stare him straight in the eye and give him a poker face. I show nothing, but nothing. Eventually, I divert my glare to his right hand as he reaches for the black receiver, his ugly hands, and then my hands.

"I can't believe it's you. Thank God. I can't believe you came to see me. Thank God. Thank God." He smiles and touches the glass to simulate touching me, my face. "Christian, you have grown into a handsome man. Look at you, all grown up!" I let his ignorance go for the moment. "You look so healthy. Last I heard, you weren't doing well, but look at you! Praise Jesus! How are you?" The tenderness in his voice reminds me of a Muppet show I wish I could forget.

"I'm fine, but you're obviously having a bad hair day."

He chuckles and pats his head. "Oh, yeah, haven't had much on top for a few years now."

I look away.

He smiles at me with a hazy expression. It reminds me of the pedophiles that sat in front of me at a recent screening of *The Heart Is Deceitful Above All Things*.

I look him straight in the eye again. It stops him mid-sentence as he's laying another compliment on me. Finally he sees me. He hears what my eyes say. They say, "I know. I remember. I know." He shuts up and swallows a gulp of saliva, looking around the visiting room to see if anyone else has "heard" my eyes. Most prisoners don't take too kindly to child molesters.

"Are you done feeding me this bullshit?"

He closes his eyes.

"I didn't come here so you could see me. I didn't come here to keep you company. I have a few things I need to say to you and then

I'm leaving." Taking a breath, I stare at my father, and he stares back like a zombie.

"I've spent my entire life searching for a way out or a way to sustain my sanity. Things were never easy for my mother or me. I didn't think much about why until I thought I murdered a man, just like you did, and it happened at a time when I couldn't even fathom life getting any worse."

He doesn't flinch. He sustains a blank expression, and the funny thing is I feel like this is his true self, empty and emotionless. I continue.

"Every day of my life I was afraid I'd end up like you, and when it finally happened, when I thought we were the same, it was like I died."

He clears his throat, and in a monotone voice replies, "I never meant to—"

"Don't say it. Don't fucking say it. It doesn't matter. You're the reason why I trust no one and love no one. You made me this way," I sob. "Drew is dead because of you."

He's very quick to defend himself. "Christian, I had nothing to do with that. Jesus Christ, he was hit by a car! You know this."

"It was bad karma. He died because of you, because you took a man's life, life was taken away from you, from us." I stifle my tears and wipe my runny nose.

"I'm sorry. You have me now. I'm a different person." The right words come out but insincerely.

"No, you're not. You're exactly the same."

Like an insubordinate child being reprimanded, he looks around the room at anything but me.

"I came here to tell you that I've changed. You can't hurt us anymore."

"I never wanted to hurt you."

I stand up as the guard comes behind my father to take him back to his home. I'm shocked as his eyes well up with tears. Our time is up.

"Christian, I'm your father."

I touch the glass with my hand. I look at him for the last time and say, "You're no father of mine."

As the guard shackles the irreparable man whose hands are full of my fury, I turn around and walk out of prison.

Michelle is sitting in the car with the radio blasting some pop song I've heard too many times. Silently, I sit down in the passenger seat and close the car door. She turns down the music and twists the key in the ignition while looking down the road.

"How do you feel?" she asks.

"Better," I say.

Christopher Stoddard was born in Connecticut in 1981. He lives in New York City. This is his first novel; he's currently working on a second. His website is whitechristianbook.com. His email address is antichrispress@gmail.com.

SPUYTEN DUYVIL
Meeting Eyes Bindery
Triton

41235894R10137

Made in the USA
Middletown, DE
07 March 2017